'Sara.'

Alex whispered her [...] have been so easy t[...] his eyes, to let his lips touch hers. But then what? All she'd striven for in the last year would have been in vain. She'd be back to square one and any thought of working alongside him, even for the brief time he'd initially suggested, would have been utterly out of the question.

Laura MacDonald lives in the Isle of Wight, and is married with a grown-up family. She has enjoyed writing fiction since she was a child, but for several years she worked for members of the medical profession, both in pharmacy and in general practice. Her daughter is a nurse and has helped with the research for Laura's medical stories.

Recent titles by the same author:

TO LOVE AND TO CHERISH*
FORSAKING ALL OTHERS*
FROM THIS DAY FORWARD*
TO HAVE AND TO HOLD*

* *The Matchmaker* quartet

VILLAGE PARTNERS

BY
LAURA MACDONALD

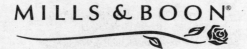

MILLS & BOON and MILLS & BOON with the Rose Device are registered trademarks of the publisher.

First published in Great Britain 1999
Harlequin Mills & Boon Limited,
Eton House, 18-24 Paradise Road, Richmond, Surrey TW9 1SR

© Laura MacDonald 1999

ISBN 0 263 81677 X

Set in Times Roman 10½ on 11½ pt.
03-9905-51757-D

Printed and bound in Norway
by AIT Trondheim AS, Trondheim

CHAPTER ONE

'WELCOME back to England, darling—it's marvellous to have you home again.'

'Thanks, it's good to be home, even if things didn't work out quite as I'd hoped.' Sara Denton took the cup of tea her aunt passed to her across the kitchen table. Outside they could hear the sound of a lawnmower as her uncle cut the grass and the occasional bark from Jason, the family Labrador, as he offered his contribution to the proceedings. They were ordinary, everyday sounds but comfortingly typical of an English summer's day.

'So, what was it that finally decided you to come home?' As Jean Rossington sat at the table and sipped her own tea, her blonde hair shone in the sunlight that streamed through the open window.

'The heat in the end, I suppose.' Sara pulled a face. 'Quite honestly, I simply couldn't stand it any longer. It's true the hospital itself was air-conditioned, but I didn't spend all my life in the hospital, and, as far as I could see, it just doesn't seem to cool down at all for very long in the Middle East.'

'Well, you gave it a good try,' said Jean. 'I've heard of people who turned around and came home almost as soon as they stepped down from the plane—at least you stuck it out for a year.'

Sara smiled. 'It wasn't all bad,' she said. 'I made some good friends and took in some very interesting places while I was there... But now...' She trailed off with a little shrug.

5

'Now you have your future to think about,' her aunt went on for her.

'Yes.' Sara nodded. 'Now I have my future to consider.'

'What about this offer of your uncle's? Have you thought about that yet?'

Instinctively they both looked out of the open doorway to the garden, where they could see Francis Rossington as he walked up and down the lawn.

'Yes.' Sara set her cup in its saucer and looped her dark hair behind her ears. 'Yes, of course, I've thought about it.'

'And?' said Jean almost eagerly.

'I think I need a bit more time,' Sara replied.

'It's a good offer,' said Jean. 'And it would be a change for you after all that hospital work.'

'Yes, it would,' Sara agreed. 'I dare say I would enjoy the work...'

'But...?' said Jean.

'But what?'

'I definitely detected a "but", coming there.' Jean paused. 'Does the family involvement bother you?'

'No.' Sara hesitated. 'No, I don't think so. There may be a few difficulties, but nothing that can't be overcome... No, it isn't that...'

'It's Alex, isn't it?'

Sara glanced up and saw that Jean was watching her shrewdly over the rim of her cup. She shifted restlessly on her chair. 'Well, Alex is certainly a factor I have to take into consideration,' she admitted at last.

'I like Alex,' said Jean. 'He's certainly fitted in very well here in the village, and his patients adore him.'

'Yes.' Sara raised one eyebrow. 'I can imagine. Alex is very charming and, when all's said and done, he's a good doctor. I would never have suggested he applied to

Uncle Francis for the job in the first place if I hadn't thought he would be suitable.' She paused, staring down into the depths of her cup.

'Well, then...' Jean spread her hands.

'What you can't get away from...' Sara took a deep breath '...is the fact that Alex and I lived together for nearly two years.'

'I know. I know, darling.' Jean looked up sharply, then gave a sigh. 'So, are you saying that fact alone would prevent you from taking up your uncle's offer?'

'I don't know.' Sara gave a quick, dismissive gesture. 'I'm not sure.'

'It would be a shame if that was the case,' Jean began.

'Well, I suppose it's inevitable it would have a bearing on it... I mean, you can't spend two years of your life with someone in an intimate relationship, then a year or so later meet up with them again and pretend none of it had ever happened.'

'I'm sure no one would expect that,' Jean replied calmly. 'It would be more a case of acknowledging the past relationship and then moving on, so to speak... Would you find that difficult?'

'Probably not.' Sara shrugged.

'I suppose, really, it depends on why you parted,' said Jean slowly.

'Alex has never said?'

'No, darling.' Jean shook her head. 'Alex has never discussed his relationship with you.'

'Oh. Oh, I see.' She was silent for a moment, reflecting, then she said, 'Well, it ended because, quite simply, it wasn't going anywhere. I felt Alex was just taking it and me for granted. When we first moved in together I was under the impression that the relationship would lead to marriage and possibly children, but as time went on

Alex seemed less and less interested in making a firm commitment.'

'What happened?' Jean leaned forward slightly.

'We had rows about it, and about that time I was offered the post in Saudi. I decided maybe what I needed was to make a fresh start.'

'It all seems so sad,' said Jean slowly. 'I used to think you made such a lovely couple.'

'Yes, well...' Sara shrugged but inside she felt the old churning feeling that thoughts of Alex still brought.

Jean was silent for a moment then she said, 'You don't think Alex's inability to commit himself had anything to do with his childhood?'

'What do you mean?' Sara looked up sharply.

'He told me about his mother, leaving when he was a boy, and of how his father was left to raise him and his brother. He said how tough it had all been. That sort of thing sometimes makes people wary of making lifetime commitments...or so I've heard.'

'Goodness knows.' Sara shrugged again. 'My parents weren't here either but that has only made me long all the more for a family of my own.'

'Ah, but the difference was that your parents loved each other,' said Jean softly.

'Yes, they did, didn't they?' Sara's voice caught in her throat, and as she thought of her parents her eyes gleamed with unshed tears.

'Has there been anyone since Alex for you?' asked Jean briskly a moment later.

'I've been out with a couple,' Sara admitted.

'But no one serious?'

'No, not really.' She paused. 'How about Alex?'

'I don't know...'

'I can't imagine Alex, living like a monk,' said Sara drily.

'Haven't you seen him since you got back?'

'No.' She shook her head.

'Well...' Jean stood and looked out of the window. 'It seems that's about to be rectified.'

'What do you mean?' Sara looked up sharply.

'He's just driven in.'

Her heart turned over and quickly she got to her feet.

'Don't go,' said Jean. 'After all, you have to see him sooner or later.'

The door opened. Alex Mason strolled from the hall into the kitchen and Sara forced herself to meet his gaze.

She had the advantage because he hadn't known she would be there but, in spite of that, she was unprepared for the shock she felt at her first sight of him. He looked exactly the same, whereas she'd been expecting him to look different in some way after a year apart. He was tall and slim, with a wide, ready smile and large expressive eyes that were neither brown nor green but a curious in-between sort of colour. His straight brown hair flopped over his forehead and he was forever pushing it back. He stood in the doorway and stared at her.

'Sara.' The brief shock of recognition in his eyes was quickly replaced by a matter-of-fact, casual sort of pleasure, which he might have extended to anyone whom he hadn't seen for a while, but it was too late because Sara had seen his initial reaction.

For the briefest of moments she was uncertain how to greet him. How did one greet an ex-live-in-lover? A kiss? A hug? A handshake maybe?

It was Alex who solved the dilemma. Moving towards her, he took both her hands in his and kissed her lightly, first on one cheek and then the other. 'It's good to see you,' he said.

'How are you, Alex?' Her response, she hoped, was

equally casual, with just the correct degree of warmth to hopefully conceal the turmoil that raged within.

'You're looking well.' He stepped back, still holding her hands, as he appeared to take in every detail, from her short haircut in its new shiny bob, her clear gray eyes, which she hoped fervently weren't betraying the havoc that was going on inside, and her lightly tanned skin.

'Yes, I am well,' she managed to say at last, 'in spite of the heat, and, yes, it is good to be home again.'

'So, where will home be exactly?' asked Alex. He spoke politely but Sara had the distinct impression he already knew.

Withdrawing her hands from his, she said briskly, 'Jean and Francis have very kindly invited me to stay here with them until I sort myself out.'

At that moment Francis himself appeared at the back door. 'Oh, it's you, Alex,' he said. 'I thought I heard a car.'

'Have you finished, dear?' asked Jean.

'Well, I've finished the grass,' said Francis, wiping his damp forehead with his handkerchief, 'but Jason is champing at the bit. He seems to think that when I switch the mower off it's a signal for a walk.'

'Maybe Sara will take him for a walk for you...' Jean began.

'Of course I will,' Sara replied. 'I could do with some exercise myself.'

'That's a good idea,' said Alex smoothly. 'I think I'll join you.'

There was nothing in the brief silence to follow that could really arouse her suspicion, but Sara was left with the distinct impression that the whole thing had somehow been contrived.

Maybe, she thought as she went to the hall cupboard to collect Jason's lead, they thought that by bringing her and Alex together again they might bring about some sort of reconciliation. Well, if that was the case they could think again. On the other hand, perhaps they thought that Alex might be able to bring pressure to bear over Francis's offer of a partnership.

This was further borne out when Sara returned to the kitchen and, amidst growing hysteria from Jason who had detected the forthcoming action, Francis turned from the sink where he was washing his hands. 'Maybe Alex will be able to twist your arm, Sara, about joining us,' he said. He caught sight of his wife's warning expression and mumbled something incoherent, before briskly wiping his hands.

'So, Saudi Arabia didn't work out?' Alex said, as they took the path at the back of the house, the path that passed between fields of ripening crops before meandering on through a copse and out onto downland.

'No.' Sara shook her head, at the same time keeping Jason on a short lead as he pulled her along, straining to be away.

'Any particular reason?' he asked. Again the question appeared casual but Sara had the feeling he knew full well the reason for her return.

'The climate was the main problem,' she replied. 'I thought I'd adjust to the heat in time, but I didn't. It was as simple as that. In the end I couldn't see any point in carrying on so I decided not to renew my contract at the end of the first year.'

'What about the work itself—did you enjoy that?' The narrowness of the pathway had forced them to walk in single file and Sara half turned to reply.

'Oh, yes, there was no problem there. I thoroughly enjoyed the work—like I say, if it hadn't been for the heat I would still be there.'

'So now you have to make new plans.' Alex paused,

and when she remained silent he said, 'Have you had time to consider Francis's offer?'

'Not really.' They had reached the stile and as she clambered over she slipped Jason's lead, allowing the dog to dart underneath before he foraged ahead, nose to the ground.

'On the surface it sounds a good solution all round,' said Alex as he swung his tall frame over the stile and joined her. 'Francis and I get a partner we know, and it solves your current situation.'

'Don't you think that if I'd wanted the life of a country GP I would have gone for it before when Francis asked me?' she said lightly.

'Instead of which, you cleared off to Saudi...'

'And you stepped in and filled the breach.' She paused, then said, 'How did it work out with you and Francis and Jim Farrow?'

'Fine, actually,' said Alex. 'It was a shock when Jim died, though, I can tell you. It knocked Francis for six.'

'It would.' Sara nodded. 'They were lifelong friends, they went through medical school together, before becoming partners and setting up the village practice. What happened?' she asked, suddenly curious. 'After Jim's death, I mean. Did you interview many others?'

'A few,' Alex admitted, 'but none of them seemed to fit the bill. Then we heard that you were coming home and Francis immediately said that maybe this time you would consider joining him. From what he's said, I gather it's always been a dream of his.'

'That's true.' Sara gave a short laugh. 'Ever since the days when I was a child and I used to play at doctors.'

'I thought all little girls wanted to be nurses.'

'Not this one. It was a doctor or nothing for me.'

'And you did it, didn't you? You got there.'

Sara nodded. 'Yes, and that was partly thanks to

Francis and Jean. They were always there for me after my parents died.'

'Maybe it would be a nice gesture if you were to realise his dream...'

'It has to be right, Alex. Not just for Francis, but for me,' she said sharply.

'But of course. I know that.' He paused again. All around them were the sounds of an ordinary English summer's day. A plane droned overhead, a bee hovered around the honeysuckle in the hedge alongside the path and from the fields around the copse could be heard the bleating of sheep. 'Are you thinking it might not be right?' he said at last. 'That it might not work out?'

'I don't know, Alex,' she said, her voice quiet now. 'I'm not sure and I don't feel it's a move I can make if it's not going to work out.'

'You'd almost decided on it once,' he said.

'I know. But that was then. That was before.'

'And is it so different now?' he said softly. They were walking side by side now because the path had widened, and as he spoke he threw her a sidelong glance.

'Of course it is, Alex.' She tried to keep the exasperation from her voice. 'You know it is.'

'All right, so tell me. What's so different?'

She stared at him, for a moment not quite certain whether he was serious or not. Jason gave a short bark and she looked up, just in time to see the dog streak away from the copse in the pursuit of something interesting, his tail wagging ecstatically.

'Everything's different, Alex,' she said tightly. 'If I'd taken up Francis's offer when he first asked me, it was at the time when you and I were still together. Now we've been parted for over a year and during that time you yourself have become a partner to Francis. It's now a totally different set of circumstances.'

'So, what you're saying is, it's me. I'm the problem.' He laughed.

'No, not entirely.' She tried to keep her voice even. 'It's the situation. To be honest, I'm not sure it would work.'

'It could work. If we let it.'

'It would have to be a completely new relationship between us, Alex—a professional one.' She hesitated. 'There would be no going back.'

'Of course not.' He spoke solemnly but when she glanced quickly at him, knowing him as well as she did, she thought she detected a hint of amusement in his eyes.

By this time they had entered the copse, cool beneath the darker green of the foliage. Their footsteps were muted on the dusty leaf-mould of the pathway and the air was heady with the scent of pine and wild garlic.

'Of course, the answer really would be a trial run, if Francis would agree,' Alex went on after a moment.

'What do you mean?'

'Well, say a month for you to work in the surgery, get to know people and see if you like it.'

'Not everyone could expect that sort of privilege.'

Alex shrugged. 'Maybe not, but you're obviously special to Francis and I'm sure he'd consider it if it meant the chance of you reaching the right decision.'

'And you'd go along with that as well?'

'Why not? There are times when I still feel bad about what happened between us, you know, Sara.'

'Alex…'

'All right, I know. No going back. But it was good, wasn't it, at the time?'

She took a deep breath. 'Yes, Alex,' she said. 'It was good. Very good. But, like you say, it's over now. It's in the past and it's time to move on.'

They walked on in silence for a while and suddenly

Sara became very aware of him as he walked at her side.
Because of the width of the pathway, which had nar-
rowed slightly again in the copse, they were almost
touching as they walked. If she let it, she could almost
imagine that it was how it had once been between them.
But if that had been the case they'd have been holding
hands, or Alex's arm would have been around her shoulders.

She mustn't think about that. She mustn't dwell on the
past or on what might have been. The future was what
mattered now.

'You can trust me, Sara,' said Alex. As he spoke he
took her arm. Because her thoughts had been running
along more intimate lines, she jumped. 'What I mean,'
he went on, 'is that I would never use our previous relationship to compromise you in any way.'

'No, Alex,' she replied, 'I know you wouldn't.' What
she didn't say was that it was herself she wasn't sure she
could trust. Her emotions had taken such a battering since
their break-up that sometimes she doubted whether she
would ever want to become that involved with anyone
again. At the same time she doubted whether she was yet
really over Alex. She couldn't imagine that working
alongside him, day in and day out, was really the best
antidote for that. He'd said he wouldn't compromise her
in any way, and by that she assumed he meant he
wouldn't take advantage of their previous relationship,
but she was wary of this.

She knew Alex too well—knew how charming, how
utterly persuasive, he could be—and at the same time she
was only too aware of her own weaknesses, especially
where Alex Mason was concerned. It would be all too
easy to allow herself to be talked round by him and once
again to find herself trapped in the same dead-end relationship which she had gone to such lengths to end.

'I'm sure we could make it work.' Alex was speaking again and Sara almost had to force herself to concentrate on what he was saying. 'And I think the idea of a month's trial would be a very good one.'

'I'm not sure I'd want to spend a whole month, just getting to know the practice,' Sara replied.

'I know,' Alex said, then he added smoothly, 'but that wasn't quite what I had in mind.'

'What, then?' She threw him a sharp glance, instinctively suspicious, but his expression gave away nothing of his intentions.

'Francis and Jean need a break,' he said. 'Francis has been working far too hard recently, especially since Jim's death, and I know Jean has been worried about him.'

'She hasn't said...' Sara frowned.

'Well, you haven't been here. Besides, she probably didn't want to worry you, but I guess Jim Farrow's death, coming so suddenly like that, has made her think. After all, Francis and Jim were the same age...'

'So, what are you proposing?' said Sara. She had the uneasy feeling that the whole thing was beginning to sound like blackmail. By this time they had come out of the coolness of the copse into bright sunlight again and were climbing the steep chalky path to the downs.

'Well, I think you would only need a week, or perhaps two, to familiarise yourself with the place,' said Alex. His tone gained momentum as he became more enthusiastic, and he went on, 'You could take over Francis's list for two or three weeks so that he and Jean could go to Canada to see David and Sue and the grandchildren—it's ages since they last went, and they haven't seen that latest child at all, you know.'

'Yes, I do know that, Alex,' she replied drily.

'Well, there you are, then. It's a wonderful solution for everyone.'

'You've got it all worked out, haven't you?' she said.

He grinned. 'It would also mean there would be some-one living in the house while they're away. You know how Jean gets nervous about that.'

'But would we be able to cope between us?' she asked dubiously, unimpressed by all this enthusiasm.

'Well, Francis and I have been coping with Jim's list,' said Alex, 'so I'm sure that you and I could cope for a few weeks. If not, I dare say we could get a locum in to give us a hand.'

He paused for breath and they stopped and looked back at the scenery behind them—the rolling Hampshire coun-tryside, the towns and villages dotted between the patch-work of fields and, in the distance, glimpses of the sea.

'Let's rest for a bit.' He indicated a natural hollow tucked beneath a grassy hillock. He whistled to Jason then eased himself down, stretching out his long legs be-fore him and folding his arms behind his head.

Sara hesitated, watching him warily, not at all sure this was what she should be doing. Jason came charging back and flopped down on the grass, his tongue hanging out and panting noisily, and she came to the conclusion that the only thing to do—if she wasn't going to look com-pletely foolish—was to join the pair of them. Carefully she sat on the grass a little way from Alex and, hugging her knees, made a show of studying the scene before them.

They were silent for a while, and the sun felt pleasantly warm on Sara's face and bare arms—not at all like the blistering heat of the sun in the Middle East.

Gradually she felt herself relax. It was good to be home again. England was at its most beautiful, and in spite of her reservations it really was very good to see Alex again. She had missed him terribly while she was away—more than she was prepared to admit, even to herself—and there was something very comforting and reassuring about sitting here beside him on this English hillside on a warm summer's afternoon.

'You can see the village from here.' Alex suddenly broke the silence, and when Sara turned her head to look at him she found he was now sitting upright and was chewing a stem of grass as he scrutinised the scene below. He looked suddenly vulnerable, younger somehow, and Sara felt the breath catch in her throat as, inevitably, memories flooded back.

Hastily she turned back to the scenery, which was far safer than giving in to nostalgia. 'Yes,' she agreed, 'and, look, there's the cathedral over there and the river.'

He leaned forward and stopped chewing the stem. 'I think I can just see my house... Yes, look, there it is amongst those trees.'

Sara frowned as it suddenly occurred to her that she hadn't a clue where he was living. 'Have you bought a house?' she asked, half turning towards him again.

'Yes, I have, as it happens—one of those cottages down near the old mill. You'll have to come and have a look at it. It's nice but very small.'

'Big enough for one, no doubt,' she said crisply.

'Oh, yes, just about big enough for one.'

'I'm amazed you find village life stimulating enough.'

He gave a short laugh. 'Believe you me,' he said darkly, 'there's more goes on in a village than in any town. Longwood Chase is no exception, as you'll find out.'

'If I choose to stay, you mean?' she said lightly.

He chose to ignore that, instead leaning forward and linking his hands between his knees. 'I've been drawn into everything since I've been here,' he said. 'As a local GP I've opened fêtes, judged baby contests, I'm on the board of governors of the local primary school and I'm on the parish council. I've taken part in sponsored charity events, I went carol-singing at Christmas and I helped organise the May ball.'

'Heavens.' Sara stared at him, momentarily lost for words at the unexpected picture he was painting. 'That doesn't sound like the Alex I know.'

'Ah,' he replied solemnly. 'Maybe the Alex you knew no longer exits.'

'Oh,' she said. She wasn't sure how she felt about that notion. In fact, she wasn't at all sure she liked the idea that the Alex she had known and loved no longer existed—that he had in some way been replaced by this paragon of virtue. In the end, she found it difficult to accept that such a transformation was even possible.

'Time to go.' Abruptly he stood and, looking down at her, held out his hand. 'I have a late surgery today.'

'Oh, I see.' She didn't really want to take the proffered hand—wasn't really sure what her body's natural response to his touch would be—but because they were sitting on such a steep slope it seemed foolhardy to decline any offer of help so, against her better judgment, she allowed him to help her to her feet.

His hand was warm, the fingers strong as they closed around hers, evoking even more memories—memories she'd hoped she'd buried deep in her subconscious, never to be resurrected. She would have withdrawn her hand immediately but, in helping her to her feet, he somehow manoeuvred it so that she ended up resting against him as she fought the contour of the slope and attempted to steady herself. Far from being released, her hand remained firmly enclosed within his own.

For a moment the power of his nearness threatened to overwhelm her—the scent of him, so reminiscent of those countless hours spent in his arms, and the warmth of his body. Briefly, in an attempt to steady herself, she leaned against him. She even felt his breath on her cheek.

'Sara.' He whispered her name just once. It would have been so easy to lift her head, to look into his eyes, to let his lips touch hers. But then what? All she'd striven for in the last year would have been in vain. She'd be back to square one and any thought of working alongside him, even for the brief time he'd initially suggested, would have been utterly out of the question.

She stiffened, pulled away from him and smartly withdrew her hand. She thought she caught the sound of a sigh, but she couldn't be certain. She called Jason and the moment was over. They began to make their way back down the steep path to the copse.

CHAPTER TWO

SARA and Alex had first met at medical school at a party given by some other students at their lodgings. Sara had immediately been attracted to the handsome young doctor who'd seemed to talk with his eyes. He'd been at the centre of an enthusiastic group who'd appeared to hang onto his every word, but he'd extricated himself from its midst and had made his way across the crowded room to her side.

'I don't believe we've met—I'm Alex Mason.'

'Sara Denton…'

From the moment he'd taken her hand—not exactly in a handshake, nothing as formal as that, but holding it for longer than he should have and looking directly into her eyes—she'd been lost. At the time she hadn't quite realised that—she'd only been aware of the frisson of excitement that had coursed through her body—but afterwards, and certainly now that it was all over, she'd realised that she'd fallen for him there and then.

They talked for hours, finding they had much in common—from their backgrounds and childhoods to their likes and dislikes. Much later, when the initial mass of students thinned out a bit and the steady thump, thump, of the music gave way to slow, smoochy, after-midnight music, they danced. He held her close and even his heartbeat seemed to match her own.

He kissed her just before the party broke up and she and her friends went back to their own digs. The following day she was in an agony of suspense until at last, at four-thirty in the afternoon, he phoned and asked her out.

They dated throughout the rest of their student days and pretty soon everyone recognised them as a couple. Sometimes she stayed over at his lodgings and sometimes he stayed with her. In the year after he qualified they finally found a flat of their own. Sara had never been happier and lived contentedly in the assumption that marriage and a family would follow.

She still wasn't certain exactly when things had started to go wrong. Looking back, she now recognised it might have been when she'd been taking her own finals and under a lot of stress but, whenever it had been, gradually Sara had realised that where she'd imagined that Alex had been ready to get married, to make that crucial commitment and settle down to family life, she'd somehow been wrong.

The final straw had come shortly after she'd qualified when she'd been considering the offer her uncle had made to her of a partnership. She'd been feeling a little off colour for a week or so and her period had been late. Gradually she'd come to suspect she might be pregnant. At first she'd been dismayed as they certainly hadn't planned a baby at that stage, but her feelings of apprehension had quickly given way to those of joy and excitement. She'd assumed Alex would have felt the same, but when she'd told him he'd been horrified.

'That's the last thing we want right now,' he said. 'You've only just qualified, for heaven's sake, and, besides, we can't afford a baby!'

'But I wouldn't be giving up my career,' she protested. 'I could return to work almost immediately.'

'And who'd look after the baby?' he demanded incredulously.

'We'd have a nanny, or at least a child-minder—'

'No child of mine will be looked after by strangers,' he cut in.

'But everyone does that these days,' she protested. 'It's normal.'

'Not for me it isn't.' His retort was sharp.

In the end it was all a false alarm. She wasn't pregnant at all. However, the whole episode left Sara amazed by the strength of her own feelings and the disappointment she'd felt when she'd discovered there'd been no baby after all. The incident opened up a source of tension between herself and Alex, which in turn led to further rows. The final quarrel led to them parting in the belief they wanted different things from life.

In Sara's need to get right away and to make a fresh start she filled in an application for a post at a hospital in Saudi Arabia. At the time it was more an act of impulsive defiance than anything else, and no one was more surprised than Sara herself when she was offered the position.

'What about your uncle's offer?' Alex demanded in disbelief when she told him of her decision.

'Perhaps you'd better take it,' she retorted.

He did—and the rest was history.

There were times, especially at first, when she bitterly regretted the rashness of her decision—times when she missed Alex so much she could hardly bear it—but slowly she learned to live without him and to get on with her life.

Now she was home and once again it seemed she was being forced to face facts and maybe yet another life-changing decision.

'So, Sara, what do you think of Alex's proposal?'

It was the following evening and the four of them were sitting in the Rossingtons' dining-room over dinner. Jean had cooked a delicious meal by way of a welcome to Sara, and it was while they were relaxing and lingering over coffee that Francis finally brought up the subject that was quite obviously in everyone's mind.

'Well,' Sara answered carefully, 'let's say it doesn't have quite such far-reaching implications as your proposal.'

Francis laughed. 'Does that make it any easier to consider?'

'Maybe it does.' Sara looked up and found that all three were watching her. Not for the first time since her return she had the feeling there was a conspiracy.

'I think it's an excellent idea,' said Francis. 'It will give you a chance, Sara, to get to know everyone—staff and patients—a chance to find out, without having to commit yourself further, whether or not you like the lifestyle.'

'And it also means,' Jean interrupted, 'that we get to go to Canada and at last I get to see my new granddaughter!'

'With a house and dog-sitter thrown in for good measure,' added Alex.

In the silence that followed the general laughter after Alex's remark Sara looked round the table. 'I'm not sure I can refuse after all that,' she said.

'Oh, Sara, that's wonderful,' said Jean.

'I don't want you to make any decision over the partnership until we get back from Canada,' said Francis, 'but I've already decided to have a word with Henry Jackson so that while we're away he can step in to do a few extra duties.'

'It looks like it's all decided, then,' said Sara with a little shrug. Across the table her gaze met Alex's. Silently she reminded herself that she'd have to make sure that he wasn't under any illusion that these arrangements were anything other than purely professional—there was no way she could cope with anything else.

*   *   *

'Come and meet the staff.' It was the following morning, and Sara and Francis had travelled together the short distance between the Rossington family home next to the church on the village green and the surgery—a long, low, purpose-built, modern building situated beside the village primary school.

Francis parked his Rover in the staff car park beside Alex's red Golf, and together he and Sara made their way inside the building.

'How many staff do you have these days?' she asked, as Francis held one of the heavy doors open for her.

'Ten,' he replied. As they approached the large semi-circular reception desk he went on, 'We have two full-time practice nurses, our practice manager, four part-time receptionists, one full-time secretary and two part-time ancillary staff who are responsible for cleaning and maintenance. There are also the community care team, who aren't actually based here but who come in on a daily basis, and our accountant, who comes in a couple of times a week and who deals with salary and wages.'

He paused and two women, who were working behind the desk, looked up as they approached. He said, 'These are two of our receptionists, Poli and Mavis. Good morning, girls. I'd like you to meet my niece, Dr Sara Denton. She'll be joining us for a little while. I'll be relying on you to help her to feel at home.'

As Sara smiled and nodded to the two girls she was aware of their surprised expressions and the glances they exchanged. She and Francis walked past the desk and the waiting area, which was already filling up, and entered a wide passage, with several rooms leading off it. The first door they reached was closed and bore the title PRACTICE MANAGER printed in black on a small mahogany plaque.

Francis tapped on the door and barely waited for a response before he turned the handle, pushed open the door and stuck his head round it. 'Oh, Geraldine, you're there,' he said. 'Good. Sorry to disturb you, but there's someone I'd like you to meet.' He turned. 'Come inside, Sara.'

As she moved into the office a tall, very attractive woman with a mass of auburn hair turned from a table where she was feeding sheets of paper into a photocopier.

'Geraldine,' Francis said, 'I'd like you to meet my niece, Dr Sara Denton. Sara, this is Geraldine Lewis, our practice manager, who's responsible for the smooth running of this place.' Sara was aware that he'd closed the door behind him. 'Geraldine,' he went on, 'it has been decided that Sara is going to join us for a while.'

'Really?' Again Sara saw the look of surprise, this time in Geraldine Lewis's eyes.

'Yes, I'm sorry we didn't have the chance to tell you before, but it's really only just been decided. Sara has recently returned to this country, after working in the Middle East.'

'Well, welcome aboard.' Geraldine nodded and smiled at Sara. 'In what capacity will you be here?'

It was Francis who answered. 'To start with, Sara will be simply familiarising herself with the practice and the general running of the surgery. Then, as soon as it can be arranged, Jean and myself are taking a trip to Canada. While we're away Sara will take over my list, if necessary, with a bit of help from Henry Jackson.'

'Does Alex know?' asked Geraldine.

'Oh, yes.' Francis laughed. 'In fact, it was Alex's idea.'

'Really?' Geraldine Lewis's eyes widened slightly and for a split second, because of the way she'd said it, Sara found herself wondering if there was anything between the practice manager and Alex. Jean had said she didn't know if Alex had been involved with anyone else or not since they'd parted, but as she, Sara, had laughingly said at the time, she couldn't imagine Alex, living the life of a monk for long.

She dismissed the thought almost at once because, after all, whatever Alex had or hadn't done while she'd been abroad could no longer be of any consequence to her.

'Alex thought it would give Sara a chance to see whether or not she likes us all,' Francis carried on.

'And if she does?' said Geraldine.

'There's a very good chance she'll opt to join us permanently,' Francis replied. 'So make sure everyone is nice to her.'

'I see,' said Geraldine. 'Well in that case, I guess we'd better get off on the right foot. Come on, Dr Denton, I'll show you around and we'll have a coffee before surgery starts.'

'Oh, please, call me Sara,' said Sara quickly, as Francis took himself off to his consulting-room.

'Very well,' said Geraldine, 'but you'll find the staff will address you as ''Doctor'' when there are any patients around—Dr Rossington is very strict about that.'

'Is he?' said Sara faintly. Somehow she couldn't imagine her uncle being strict about anything but, then, she'd never really observed him in the workplace. Maybe he was very different from how he appeared at home.

'Yes.' Geraldine nodded. 'He also doesn't go along with the modern practice these days of calling patients by their first names—unless it happens to be someone he's known for a long time.'

'I would have thought that was most people in a place like Longwood Chase,' Sara replied.

'How long is it since you've been here?'

'Well, I was abroad for a year and before that it was only really fleeting visits—you know, Christmas and other family occasions, that sort of thing—but I did spend quite a bit of time here when I was a child with my cousins, David and Hillary.'

'I think you'll find there have been a lot of changes since then.' Geraldine pulled a wry expression. 'Not all for the better either. Come on, I'll show you around.' Opening the door, they stepped out into the corridor.

'What sort of changes?' asked Sara.

'Well, for a start, the property developments.'

'Oh, yes, Jean, my aunt, was saying something about that. Isn't there a big housing estate…?'

'There are two,' said Geraldine. 'One up at Carter's Fields and the other at The Spinney. Most of our patients come from there these days, hence the need for the extra partner.'

'The village itself doesn't look any different from how I always remembered it.'

'That's true,' Geraldine agreed. 'At least the planners have left that alone.' She paused as they passed an open door. 'Staffroom in there,' she said, 'with facilities beyond. And down here…' she carried on walking '…are the other two consulting-rooms. One was Dr Farrow's and this is Dr Mason's.' Lifting her hand, she knocked on the door. Alex bade them enter, and as she opened the door she said, 'I gather you've met Dr Mason?'

'Yes, Geraldine.' It was Alex who answered, Alex who stood up from behind his desk to greet them. 'Yes, Sara and I have met.'

Sara threw him a quick glance. It seemed a strange thing to say—simply that they'd met—when the reality was that they'd actually once lived together. She didn't, however, contradict him. Somehow it didn't seem the right thing to do in front of a member of his staff, but at the same time it fuelled the earlier curiosity she'd felt about the two of them.

'I'm not sure what the procedure is going to be,' said Geraldine. 'Dr Rossington said you needed to get to know the place.' She looked at Sara. 'Will you be taking surgeries straight away?'

'I'm not sure,' Sara replied. Looking at Alex, she said, 'What did you have in mind, Alex?'

'I thought just generally familiarising yourself with the place for the first few days. Sit in on surgeries, mine and Francis's, and come with us on house calls. See how the nurses operate their clinics and how the admin system works. Then, when you're ready, you could use Jim's room, and for starters do a few extra surgeries on your own—what do you say?'

'Sounds OK to me,' said Sara.

'Is that all right with you, Geraldine?' Alex asked, with his most charming smile.

'Well, yes, yes, of course it is,' Geraldine replied. 'I'd better go and brief the girls and tell them what's going on.' She paused and looked at them both, as if uncertain what would happen next.

'That's an excellent idea,' said Alex smoothly. 'Maybe you could arrange some coffee for Sara and myself before we start.'

Geraldine looked faintly bemused. 'You mean Sara will sit in with you this morning?'

Alex nodded, then said briskly, 'There's no time like the present, Geraldine. She has to start somewhere.'

'Yes, of course.' With her head down the practice manager hurried from the room.

As the door closed behind her Sara looked at Alex. 'She doesn't know about us, does she?'

Alex shook his head.

'You didn't want her to know, did you?'

'No.'

'Why not?'

'I don't think it's a good idea that any of the staff knows,' said Alex calmly.

'I don't see what the problem is.'

'There's no problem. I just happen to think it better if they don't know. There's quite enough gossip in the village, without us adding to it.'

'I can't see what there is to gossip about. We had a relationship. We lived together—plenty of people do. We parted. End of story.'

'Exactly. As you keep reminding me, it's over—in the past. I happen to think it would arouse unnecessary speculation, especially amongst the staff, if they were to be told that we'd once been an item. There's nothing they love better than a good old speculate over their morning coffee and chocolate Bourbons. Honestly, Sara, it wouldn't be fair to you. It would be putting you at an unfair disadvantage. I can take it, hide like a rhinoceros...'

'OK. Point taken.' Sara was sensitive and she knew Alex knew that. 'But you'd better warn Francis because he's more than likely to put his foot in it.'

'I've already had a word with Francis and told him that I thought it best if our past relationship wasn't mentioned.'

'Oh. What did he say?'

'When I pointed out the reasons he agreed wholeheartedly with me. Ah...' He looked up as the door opened again. 'Good, here's our coffee. Thank you, Poli.'

He was being touchy, Sara told herself as she sipped her coffee, because she'd made it plain that their relationship was purely a professional one now. So touchy, in fact, that he wasn't even prepared to admit they'd had a relationship. All that about speculation and gossip among the staff was an excuse and a pretty poor one at that. No, this was simply retaliation. Well, two could play at that game. And there she'd been, thinking he might have been planning to resume their relationship. It just showed how wrong she'd been over that one.

At that moment the intercom buzzed on the desk and when Alex flicked the switch a voice said, 'Sorry to interrupt, Dr Mason, but are you ready to start yet? Folk are getting rather restless out here.'

Alex glanced at his watch. 'Yes, Mavis, I dare say they are. I'm ten minutes late. Right, who do we have first?'

'It's Mrs Turvey, Doctor. You do have the notes. I put them on your desk.'

'Right. Thank you, Mavis. Oh, Mavis, is Mrs Turvey alone?'

'No, Dr Mason. She has Grant and Liam with her.'

'So…'

'She made a triple appointment, Doctor.'

Alex sighed. 'All right, Mavis. Send them in.' As he flicked the intercom switch again he gave Sara a rueful glance. 'I would say you're about to have a baptism of fire,' he said.

'Sounds ominous. So who exactly are the Turveys?'

'They're a family from the Carter's Fields estate.'

'Sounds as if they're a bit notorious.'

'They were rehoused here from an inner-city area. Let's just say they haven't found the transition quite what they thought it might be,' said Alex. 'Oh, here we go. Come in,' he called, in response to a knock on the door.

Linda Turvey, a thin, sallow-faced woman who appeared to have her whole turbulent life history etched on her face, came into the room, pushing one child in front of her and dragging the second behind her.

'Good morning, Mrs Turvey,' said Alex. 'Take a seat, please.'

The boys, who appeared to be around nine or ten years of age, had hair cropped so closely that at first glance their heads looked shaven. They wore coloured shell suits and both had gold studs in their ears.

'What can I do for you?' asked Alex, looking from Linda to the two boys—one of whom was kicking the edge of the carpet with the toe of his black trainers. 'No school today?'

'No, that's why they're here...' Linda Turvey trailed off and turned her head to glare suspiciously at Sara.

'This is Dr Denton, Mrs Turvey,' said Alex. 'She's visiting the practice for a while. Do you have any objection to her sitting in on this consultation?'

'I suppose not.' The woman eyed Sara up and down, apparently taking in every detail from her neatly bobbed dark hair to the crisp white shirt she wore under her dark green suit. 'You say she's a doctor?'

'Yes,' said Alex patiently, 'she's a doctor.'

'So she's qualified?'

'She's every bit as qualified as I am.'

'Well, in that case, I suppose it won't do no harm.'

Sara shifted slightly in her chair, a little irritated at this dialogue which was taking place as if she were invisible.

'So, what's wrong with you boys?' Alex turned his attention to the older of the boys who'd sat down and was staring at the floor. 'Grant?'

'He says he's been sick this morning,' said Linda Turvey. Turning to the younger boy and raising her voice, she said, 'Liam, stop kicking that carpet—you'll ruin those trainers. I've only just bought them, and you won't get another pair if you go through the toes.'

'When were you sick, Grant?' asked Alex, standing and moving round the desk until he was standing in front of the boy.

'When I got up,' muttered Grant Turvey, without looking up.

'Do you think it might have been something you'd eaten?' suggested Alex.

'More like something he'd drunk,' sniggered the younger boy.

'What d'you mean?' Linda Turvey swung round on Liam. When the boy refused to volunteer any more information she reverted to her elder son once more. 'Grant!' she yelled. 'You been drinking again? I told you before. If I find you have, I'll kill you. God help you. I will.' She looked at Sara. 'I'll kill him. Making me bring you here, wasting Dr Mason's time. I'm sorry, Doctor.'

'Have you been drinking, Grant?' asked Alex quietly.

The boy didn't answer at once and there was silence in the consulting-room, apart from the sound of Liam as he resumed his kicking of the carpet.

'Grant?' prompted Alex.

'It were only some lager,' muttered the boy, instinctively ducking, as if he was anticipating his mother's reaction to this admission.

'I'll give him lager—Liam, will you stop that kicking!'

'You have to learn two things, Grant,' said Alex. 'One is that you are too young to drink alcohol, and the other is that if you do drink it there's a good chance it'll make you sick. Now, what about you, Liam? I gather you have a problem as well.'

'He's got a sore throat—or so he says. Show the doctor your throat, Liam,' ordered his mother.

Mercifully the kicking stopped as the boy stood up and in a bored fashion opened his mouth, without waiting for Alex to even approach him.

'Yes,' said Alex a moment later, after he'd taken a tongue depressor from the desk and examined the boy's throat and glands, 'there is some infection there. How long have you had this, Liam?'

'About a week.' The boy shrugged. 'It keeps coming back.'

'Do you get a cold after these sore throats?'

'Well, do you?' demanded his mother. Looking up at Alex, she went on, 'I lose track which of the kids have colds—they all seem to have snotty noses all the time.'

'I haven't had a cold,' said Liam. 'I only get a sore throat.'

'Well, I'll prescribe you a course of antibiotics to clear it up,' said Alex, returning to his desk, 'but I want to see you again when you've finished the course. Is that clear, Mrs Turvey? I want you to make another appointment for Liam for a week's time. Maybe you could do that on the way out. Now, is there anything else?'

'Yes, it's my turn now,' Linda Turvey replied. 'Go on, you kids, clear off and wait in the waiting room. I won't be long.' As the boys went out of the room she looked at Sara and said, 'I don't intend to discuss my private bits in front of them.'

'No, quite,' Sara replied faintly, wondering if Linda Turvey was prepared to discuss private matters in front of her.

'Right, Mrs Turvey,' said Alex, 'what can I do for you?'

'I went for a smear,' she said obviously considering that Sara's qualifications were sufficient. 'And I had a letter to say I had to come and see you.'

'Ah, yes,' said Alex. He took a wad of letters from the woman's notes and scanned the most recent one. 'Yes, indeed. Now, according to your smear result, you have an infection.'

'You mean cancer, don't you?' demanded Linda. Sara looked up sharply at the dull, resigned note in the woman's voice.

'No, Mrs Turvey,' said Alex firmly, 'I do not mean

cancer. I said an infection, and I meant an infection. I've
treated you for thrush in the past and this infection is
very similar to that. I'll prescribe some tablets and pes-
saries for you to use.

'Now, let me see...' He glanced at the computer
screen, which showed Linda's medication chart. 'You're
still using the Pill for contraception, aren't you?'

'I'm not coming off that so you needn't bother even
suggesting it.'

'I wasn't going to suggest it,' replied Alex. 'What I
was about to say was that your...partner will also need
a course of tablets.'

'What for?' demanded Linda.

'Well, there's a good chance that you'll pass this infection backwards and forwards between you so he needs
to be treated at the same time as you.'

'You try telling him that.' She gave a short, humour-
less laugh.

'Is he my patient?' asked Alex.

'No, Dr Rossington's.'

'In that case, I suggest he makes an appointment to
see Dr Rossington and explains the situation to him so
that he can receive the appropriate medication. It'll go
on and on, Mrs Turvey, if you don't.'

'Well, I'll tell him.' Linda took the prescription that
Alex handed to her and stood. 'But I don't for one minute
think he will.' She'd reached the door by now but she
paused with one hand on the handle and looked back at
Alex and Sara. 'Even if he does, what about his wife?'

'What about his wife?' asked Alex faintly.

'Well, no one's going to tell her, are they?' With that
she was gone, banging the door behind her.

'Phew!' said Sara softly. 'Is that a typical example of
your list?'

'I did warn you,' said Alex ruefully. 'Do you think you're up to this?'

'Oh, I'm not complaining,' said Sara. 'I shall look on it as a challenge.'

'Good,' said Alex, 'because it's more than likely that the younger boy's sore throat is a direct result of glue-sniffing. I did warn you, didn't I,' he added when he caught sight of her expression, 'that village life is far from dull?'

CHAPTER THREE

'I HAVE to visit old Matt Jenkins,' said Alex later, 'but we'll do that after we've been down to The Spinney.'

'I remember old Mr Jenkins,' said Sara. 'When we were kids he used to chase us off the farmland. He'd worked down at Morris's farm for as long as anyone could remember. Does he still live down there?'

'Yes.' Alex nodded as he drove out of the staff car park. 'The Morris place went to rack and ruin after old Mr Morris died but somehow old Matt still lives in the same farm cottage. His health isn't so good these days, though.'

'How old is he now?'

'No one seems to know, but he must be in his eighties.'

'What's wrong with him?'

'Arthritis mainly. He simply can't get about any more, but at the same time he's reluctant to admit it.'

It was lunchtime and as Alex drove past the school the cries and shouts of the children at play drifted through the open window of the car.

'You said we're going to The Spinney first?' asked Sara. 'That's another new development, isn't it?'

'Yes. You'll find it a bit different from Carter's Fields but I don't suppose the problems of the patients are much different.'

'Who are we visiting?'

'A young lady called Mandy Richardson.'

'And what's her problem?'

'Not really a problem,' said Alex. 'A new baby.'

'That's nice,' said Sara, deliberately keeping her tone light. 'Boy or girl?'

'A little girl—Bethany,' Alex replied, his tone equally as light. 'They are fairly new patients. Husband Duncan is an architect and has his office in Petersfield. Mandy was in advertising and worked for a company in London.'

Sara wanted to ask if the patient was going to continue with her job now that she had the baby but somehow she couldn't quite bring herself to do so. That was too close to the problems she and Alex had had and one of the reasons which had led the break-up of their own relationship. Instead, she turned her attention to the leafy, partly wooded area they were now approaching, with glimpses of large houses just visible through the trees.

'This is the one,' said Alex, as he turned the car into a wide driveway set with neat pink paving-stones. 'Woodsmoke.'

The front door was opened by a middle-aged woman, who turned out to be Mandy Richardson's mother and who'd come to stay with her daughter for a few days following the birth.

'Come in, Doctor,' the woman said, her gaze flickering questioningly to Sara. After Alex had made the necessary introductions they followed her up the thickly carpeted stairs to the master bedroom, where they found Mandy, sitting up in bed against a mountain of pillows and feeding her baby. By the side of the bed was an expensive-looking cradle trimmed with a frilled canopy and valance in white broderie anglaise.

'Hello, Mandy. Congratulations, and well done.' Alex leaned over the bed and gently touched the baby's downy head.

'Thank you, Dr Mason.' Mandy smiled, but Sara noticed she looked exhausted. Her hair was lank, there were dark smudges under her eyes and her face looked red and blotchy.

'Mandy, this is Dr Denton,' said Alex casually. 'She's doing house calls with me today.'

It was Sara who saw the alarm in Mandy's eyes. 'Hello, Mandy,' she said. 'Don't mind me—there's no problem. I'm simply familiarising myself with the area. May I see the baby?'

Mandy nodded and, moving closer, Sara watched for a moment as the baby nuzzled at her mother's breast.

Since her break-up with Alex, Sara had tried to convince herself that she wasn't interested any more in the idea of having children. She therefore found herself surprised by the force of emotion that suddenly flooded over her. 'Dr Mason tells me you're calling her Bethany,' she said, as she struggled to regain her composure. 'That's nice. I like that.'

'I wasn't sure at first,' Mandy's mother said from the doorway, 'but I have to say the name's growing on me. She looks just like Mandy did when she was born.'

'When did you get home from hospital?' asked Sara, turning to Mandy again.

'Two days ago,' Mandy replied.

'And you're coping?' said Alex.

'Yes,' said Mandy, then correcting herself, said, 'Well, Mum is.'

'How long are you able to stay?' Alex turned to Mandy's mother.

'For a week,' she replied. 'Then Duncan is taking a week's holiday.'

'And after that I'll be on my own.' Mandy pulled a face.

'You'll be fine,' said Sara reassuringly. 'I'm sure you will.'

'I don't know,' said Mandy. 'At this rate I'll be glad

to get back to work. There's more to this baby lark than
anyone ever led me to believe. Take this, for example.'
She glanced down at the baby. 'I thought babies were
born, knowing how to suck. Bethany wasn't. She still
hasn't got the hang of it.'

'Don't let her make you sore,' said Sara.

'Has the midwife been in this morning?' asked Alex.

'Yes.' Mandy nodded. 'She bathed Bethany. And she's
asked the health visitor to call.'

'She'll help with any feeding problems,' said Sara.
'Tell her about Baby, not sucking properly— Oh sorry,
Dr Mason,' she added hastily, as Alex, his eyebrows
raised, looked over his shoulder at her. 'Mandy is your
patient and here's me, going on...'

'Not at all, Dr Denton,' said Alex smoothly. 'I sometimes think us men are very out of place at a lady's lying-
in.'

'I haven't heard that expression for years.' Mandy's
mother gave a laugh. 'Not since my grandmother's day.'

'Ah, but I guarantee you all knew what it meant,' said
Alex, with a quick smile at the three women. 'Now, while
this young lady's making up her mind whether she wants
to feed or not I'd like to take a quick look at the cord.'

Sara, Mandy, and her mother all watched as Alex
gently lifted the baby from her mother's breast amidst
little mewling sounds of protest. 'She may not be sucking
correctly,' said Alex, 'but she sure objects to be taken
away from her mum.' Carefully he laid the baby on the
bed and undid the poppers down the front of the tiny
white Babygro she was wearing.

'That looks fine,' he said a moment later, after examining the remains of the umbilical cord.

'The midwife gave us some powder to use if it looks
sticky at all,' said Mandy, leaning forward anxiously.

'Good.' Alex refastened the poppers, then straightened. 'So, that's baby sorted out. Now, what about her mum?'

'Oh, I'm all right,' said Mandy. 'I didn't realise I could actually feel this tired and still be awake but, other than that, I'm OK.'

'Are you eating well?'

'Oh, yes. Mum sees to that.'

'Still taking your iron tablets?'

'Yes.'

'Bowels OK?'

'Er...not really.'

'Right, let's sort that out, then.' Alex reached for his case and took out a prescription pad, leaving Mandy's mother to pick up her granddaughter, who by this time was dozing, and put her back into her cradle.

Sara watched. She was still fighting an almost uncontrollable wave of emotion which, she told herself, was quite ridiculous. She was a doctor, for heaven's sake, and she should be used to this sort of thing. If she wasn't— because her work in hospitals hadn't really brought her into much contact with nursing mothers and babies—then she jolly well had better get used to it and stop being so sentimental if she intended to pursue life as a GP.

Almost as if she'd read her thoughts, Mandy's mother turned from the cradle, looked at Sara and said, 'Are you married, Doctor?'

'No,' said Sara quickly, taken unawares. 'No, I'm not.'

'So you still have all this to come?'

'Well, yes. Yes, I suppose I have.' To her confusion Sara looked up to find that Alex had paused in writing the prescription and was looking up at her over the lid of his open case.

Helplessly she met his gaze, powerless for a moment to look away. Suddenly, hot on the heels of the emotion she had just felt at the sight of the newborn baby, a fresh rush of feeling took its place and mentally she was back with Alex, the way they'd once been. Back to the time when they'd loved each other, wanted each other and had planned for a future—a future that could have included children just like the one that slept now in the cradle, her tiny hands tightly clasped beneath her chin.

Sara didn't know what Alex was thinking, but after they'd left the house they were both very quiet on the drive to Matt Jenkins's farm cottage.

The front door was on the latch. They called out and Alex let them in. They found Matt seated in an upright chair by the fireplace in his living-room. In spite of the fact that it was summer, the gas fire was burning.

'Hello, Matt,' said Alex cheerfully. 'How are we today?'

'Well, I don't know how you are, but I'm bloody awful,' grumbled the old man. 'I can hardly get out of this chair me rheumatism's so bad and if that ain't enough...I'm having trouble with indigestion now.' He turned his head to look at Alex and as he did so he caught sight of Sara. 'Hello,' he said, his eyes narrowing. 'Who's this?'

Before Alex could answer Sara stepped forward. 'Hello, Matt,' she said. 'It's Sara Denton, Dr Rossington's niece. Do you remember me? I used to come here in the school holidays and play with David and Hillary.'

'I remember, all right,' said Matt, eyeing her up and down. 'Cheeky little bit you were an' all...always trespassing on Morris land, if I remembers rightly.'

'I was only a child, Matt,' protested Sara, aware of Alex's amused grin.

'Well, let's hope you've changed your ways...and it's Mr Jenkins to you, young lady. That's the trouble with kids today.' Matt Jenkins looked up at Alex. 'No respect for their elders.'

'Absolutely,' said Alex solemnly. Catching sight of Sara's expression, he said, 'Actually, Matt, Sara is a doctor now.'

'Eh?' Matt peered up at Sara. 'Doctor, you say? Oh, well, that figures, I suppose... She were a bossy kid as well. We had another lady doctor here once—she were bossy an' all.'

'Yes, quite, Matt,' said Alex. Sara knew he was struggling to keep a straight face. 'But now can we talk about your indigestion?'

'Burns, it does,' said the old man. 'Comes right up in my throat and burns, just like caustic soda.'

'In that case I'm going to prescribe an antacid for you to take before meals,' said Alex. 'I'm also going to change the tablets I last prescribed for your arthritis.'

'Why?' Matt peered suspiciously at Alex. 'D'you think they might be giving me indigestion?'

'It's possible,' said Alex as he consulted Matt Jenkins's medical file.

'Fat lot of good they were, then,' said Matt contemptuously.

'Did they help with your joint pains?' asked Alex.

'They might have done,' said Matt cagily. 'But what good is that if they just bring on another load of trouble.'

'That's what we're trying to sort out,' said Alex.

'What if these new ones don't help? Or if they start up more trouble? What then? That's what I want to know,' demanded Matt.

'Do you use TENS machines here?' Sara looked at Alex.

'Sometimes, yes,' he said, 'if drug intolerance is high. We could try one, if Matt agrees.'

'Eh, what's all this?' Matt looked startled. 'I'm not going nowhere. I don't want no hospitals.'

'You wouldn't have to go anywhere, Matt,' explained Alex. 'A TENS machine could be brought here for you to use at home to help relieve your pain.'

'A machine, you say?'

'They can be very effective, Mr Jenkins,' said Sara.

'I don't want no newfangled machinery,' said Matt, a stubborn expression coming over his face. 'I reckons most of the trouble in this world is caused by newfangled machinery. You take farming and the state it's in today. Go back to the old ways—that's what I say. That way there'd be plenty of work for everyone.'

'All right, Matt.' Alex tore off the prescription and handed it to him. 'I've prescribed some medicine for your heartburn and some different tablets for you to try for your pain. I expect your daughter will be in later. She'll get your prescription for you.'

'She might not.' A whining note had entered Matt's voice. 'She don't come in every day.'

'She will today,' said Alex. 'She was the one who phoned and asked me to visit so she knows there'll be a prescription to collect. I'll call in and see you again in a week or so. Goodbye, Matt.'

They turned to leave but had barely reached the door when Matt Jenkins spoke again. 'You at the surgery permanent now?' he said curiously.

Sara paused, guessing the question had been directed at her. 'I'm there for a while,' she said. 'After that, we'll have to see.'

'Going to take Dr Farrow's place, are you?'

'Nothing's been decided yet,' said Sara.

'That were sudden, him keeling over like that,' said Matt. 'Just goes to show you, doesn't it? If that can happen to the likes of him—him being a doctor and all that—

what hope is there for the rest of us? That's what I want to know.'

As they got into the car Alex suddenly chuckled. 'Are you enjoying your morning?' he asked.

'Let's say it's been interesting,' said Sara, taking a deep breath. 'So, where to next?'

'Back to the surgery. Time for a spot of lunch before the afternoon list. No, wait a minute. On second thoughts,' said Alex, 'there's something I'd like you to see.'

She threw him a questioning glance as, on reaching the top of the bumpy lane where Matt Jenkins lived, Alex turned the car to the left and not to the right as he would have done had he intended to return to the surgery.

'I thought you might like to see where I live,' he said.

'Yes,' she replied, 'I would. Didn't you say it was one of the old mill cottages?'

'That's right. I'm rather pleased with it. I've done most of the renovations myself.'

'You?' She stared at him in astonishment.

He gave a short laugh. 'Do you find that so unbeliev-able?'

'Yes, I do, actually. If I remember rightly, when we were in the flat it was as much as I could do to get you to paint around that window-frame. And when I asked you to emulsion the kitchen ceiling I could have been excused for thinking it was the end of the world.'

He grinned. 'I told you I'd changed, didn't I?'

'Yes, you did. But I'm getting really concerned now—I hadn't expected quite such a drastic personality trans-formation.'

'Ah, you'd be surprised,' he said. 'Well, here we are.' He brought the car to a halt before the row of tiny pastel-washed cottages which had once been a part of the old flour mill. Masses of flowers bloomed in tubs and baskets in front of the cottage doors—geraniums, deep blue trailing lobelia, pansies with velvet faces and waxy-petalled busy Lizzie.

Inside the cottage the rooms, although low-ceilinged and small, had retained the original oak beams and against one whitewashed wall was a black-leaded kitchener.

'Oh, Alex, it's lovely!' Sara stared around her in awe.

'If you decide to stay in Longwood Chase,' he said, leaning against the back of a chair with his arms folded as he watched her prowl around, 'you may be interested in the fact that the cottage next door is also on the market.'

'Is it?' She swung around eagerly, her eyes shining before reality set in.

'Maybe you could put an offer in.' He winked. 'There's nothing better, to my mind, than knowing who your neighbors are.'

'I don't know, Alex,' she said dubiously. 'Maybe that wouldn't be such a good idea.'

'I don't see why not.' He shrugged and, pushing himself away from the chair, went on, 'If we're going to be working together, I can't see any reason why we shouldn't live near one another.'

'We might find it restrictive,' said Sara lightly.

'In what way?' He raised his eyebrows.

'In that each of us may feel the other is keeping an eye on them.'

'I suppose that rather depends on what you intend to get up to.' He laughed. 'Perhaps it would bother you if I were to see your many boyfriends.'

'I should be so lucky.' Sara pulled a face. 'On the other hand, I could say the same thing. Would you want me, spying on your activities?'

'Speaking of which, would you like to see the bed-rooms?' he went on.

'How many do you have?' she asked calmly, choosing to ignore the obviousness of the innuendo.

'Only two. Come on, come and see.' He led the way up the narrow staircase in the corner of the sitting-room, ducking under the low beam.

'Have you hit your head on that?' she asked as she followed him.

'Yes,' he replied, 'but I assure you it's something you only do once. I nearly knocked myself out.'

'It's a wonder it didn't put you off the place.'

'I think it would take much more than that.'

'I have to admit, it really is charming,' Sara agreed, as a moment later she stood beside Alex in the main bed-room under the eaves of the cottage and looked around her. The double bed was neatly made and covered with a patchwork quilt. In one corner stood an old-fashioned washstand, complete with a blue and white bowl and jug, while beneath a rocking chair in front of the window was a pair of Alex's shoes.

On the bedside table stood the silver-framed photo-graph of his father which had been beside the bed in their flat. Without a word she went and picked it up, and for some time stood there, staring down at it, her thoughts a jumble of mixed emotions.

'It's not quite as primitive as it looks,' said Alex at last, breaking into her thoughts. 'There's a shower-room through there.'

It was only as she replaced the photograph and looked up that she realised she had a lump in her throat. It was all so familiar yet at the same time so alien—as if these objects had all been part of another life.

Dutifully she looked at the shower-room which, in spite of careful renovation, still looked too modern, and at the second bedroom, so small that it was little more than a box-room.

As Alex waited for her to lead the way downstairs once more she found herself pausing in the bedroom doorway, her gaze drawn back into the room as if hypnotised by what she saw there.

'It seems strange now, doesn't it?' he said quietly, as if he'd read her thoughts.

'Yes,' she agreed, instinctively knowing what he meant. 'It does.'

'Sometimes it's like it was only yesterday when we were together but…' He hesitated and that boyish, vulnerable look which she knew so well crossed his features. 'There are other times when I feel it was so long ago it was in another lifetime.'

This so exactly echoed her own thoughts that for a moment the accuracy of his analysis shocked her, and all she could do was stare helplessly back at him.

'It would be so easy, wouldn't it?' he said softly, leaning forward so that his face was only inches from her own. Again her senses were assailed by all the old feelings and sensations. 'To just slip back to the way we were. To pretend the last year never was.'

He was right, of course—it would be easy. It would be so easy to pretend that everything was the way it had once been between them—to have him take her into his arms, undress her, slip beneath that quilt and let him make love to her, just like he used to do.

For one brief, wild moment Sara closed her eyes and allowed her imagination to run riot. She could feel the touch of his skin against hers, the hardness of his body, the slight roughness of his jaw against the soft skin of her face, the delicious anticipation followed by the sweet thrill of the moment when he took her and they became one.

And that was what had been so hard to bear, what had made their parting so painful—the fact that they had become one. If she were tempted to let it all happen again she'd have all that pain to deal with again when it came to nothing—as it surely would because there was nothing to indicate that Alex had changed his views in any way.

'No, Alex.' The intensity of her thoughts made her tone more sharp than it might have been, leaving him in no doubt of her decision. With a half-angry little gesture that left him with a bemused expression on his face she brushed him aside and clattered noisily down the staircase, leaving him to follow more slowly.

Maybe it was what he wanted. Maybe he could cope with it. No doubt it wouldn't affect him. But it was the last thing she could allow to happen.

If she did decide to take up the partnership and stay in Longwood Chase, it would be how she'd spelt it out to him at the beginning—a purely professional arrangement. As for the idea of her buying the next door cottage to him, well, that was so ludicrous it wasn't even worth considering.

For the next week Sara continued to familiarise herself with the running of the Longwood Chase Practice. She sat in on more of Alex's surgeries and a few of Francis's, getting to know the patients and what sort of problems typified a normal week. She accompanied both men on house calls, combining her previous knowledge of the geography of the area with the new experience of the recent property developments.

Several times house calls took them up to Carter's Fields, the large housing estate to the north of the village. The residents there were a mix of people—from those like the Turveys, who'd been rehoused from inner-city areas, to locals who could no longer afford to live in the newly renovated and much-desired properties in and around the village.

There were, inevitably, many young people on the estate, but with unemployment high there was little for them to do. The social problems that resulted from this—the abuse of alcohol and a growing drugs situation—put enormous strains on the medical resources.

'It makes me feel so helpless,' said Francis on one occasion as they drove through the estate, having visited a patient with severe emphysema from his years of employment in heavy industry. 'You can see the problems before they develop, but there's so little anyone can do about them.'

'Did these people want to come here to live?' asked Sara, looking out of the car window at a group of youths who were lounging against a graffiti-covered wall.

'Some of them might have done in the first place,' Francis replied. 'It probably sounded wonderful—all that fresh air and country living after the dust and grime of the cities—but the reality can be very different. Many of them don't understand the countryside. Young families are cut off from their relatives, who in the past may have provided back-up with child-care or advice when things went wrong.

'There's even less work here than they had before and most of them, especially the young, are bored out of their minds. In this climate it's inevitable that the crime rate has risen.

'I'm sure you can remember, Sara, when you were a child and used to stay here. No one bothered to lock their doors—you couldn't do that now.'

'I thought you were trying to persuade me to stay.' Sara pulled a face. 'If you carry on like that you'll be putting me right off.'

'It's a strange thing, you know.' Francis Rossington

sighed. 'In spite of what I've just told you, I still love this place and I wouldn't want to live anywhere else. There's nothing more beautiful than the countryside around Longwood Chase.'

'What will you do after you retire?'

'We have no plans to move, if that's what you mean.'

'Well, that certainly has to say something.'

'I hope you'll decide to join us,' said Francis a little later as he drove into the car park of the medical centre. He paused, and as he switched off the engine he said, 'And I also hope that working with Alex isn't a problem for you in view of your previous relationship with him.'

Sara took a deep breath. 'No,' she said, 'no, it isn't a problem.'

Francis seemed to heave a sigh of relief. 'Oh, I'm so glad,' he said. 'Jean was concerned that it might be but, knowing you as I do, I thought you'd be mature enough to cope with it.'

'And what about Alex?' said Sara as they got out of the car.

'Oh, I wasn't worried about Alex. He takes everything in his stride. No, it was you I was concerned about, Sara, but now you say there's no problem then everything's absolutely fine.'

'Yes,' said Sara faintly, 'absolutely fine.' If only, she thought as she followed him inside the building, if only...it were that simple.

CHAPTER FOUR

'FANCY a spot of lunch later, Sara?' Geraldine Lewis placed the morning mail on Sara's desk.

'Yes, I'd like that, Geraldine.' Sara smiled up at the practice manager.

'Fine. We'll go up to the pub when you've finished your house calls.' Geraldine paused. 'So, how's it all going?'

'Pretty well...I think. At least it was while Dr Rossington was here. It could be a different story now that he's gone.'

'Don't worry,' said Geraldine with a sympathetic smile. 'I'm sure everything will work out all right. You must tell me if you find things are getting too much. I've had strict instructions from Dr Rossington that I have to call in Dr Jackson if need be.'

'Thanks, Geraldine, I really don't know what I'd do without you.'

'Don't mention it.' Geraldine laughed and went out of the room, leaving Sara with a mountain of mail that required her attention.

It was true, she thought as the door closed behind Geraldine, the practice manager really had put herself out to assist Sara in any way she could. Now it seemed that, with the offer of lunch, she was also offering the hand of friendship. Sara was glad about that because, apart from Alex, she didn't really know anyone else, and now that Jean and Francis had left for Canada she could have felt quite lonely.

Not that she had that much time to feel lonely. Work

took up most of each day—surgeries, clinics, house calls and staff meetings—leaving her so exhausted that by each evening she was glad to return to the house, to take Jason for a run, before eating supper and falling into bed. In spite of this, she was enjoying the work and found it satisfying yet demanding.

She had also been quite wrong in thinking there might have been something between the practice manager and Alex. There had been nothing since that first day when she'd witnessed Geraldine's surprise at it having been Alex's suggestion that Sara joined the practice for a while. Not a look, a smile or anything in their conversation implied a relationship other than that between employer and employee.

She worked steadily through the morning's list, with its usual assortment of seasonal ailments—hayfever, other allergies and a crop of sport-induced injuries as the tennis and cricket seasons got underway.

The patients she was seeing were mainly from Francis Rossington's list and most were old residents of Longwood Chase. Some of them remembered Sara from her childhood visits.

'Doesn't seem possible,' said one of these, Betty Collins. She was the last patient on the morning's list and had come for a blood-pressure check and medication review. 'I can't believe you're a doctor now. You and young David Rossington were a fine pair of scallywags, I recall—always in some scrape or another—while that little sister of his used to tag on behind and follow the pair of you everywhere.'

'I know.' Sara laughed. 'And now David's a top surgeon in Toronto and Hillary is a paediatrician.'

'She's in Scotland, isn't she?' Betty Collins went on. Not waiting for Sara's reply, she added, 'That's nice for the doctor and Mrs Rossington—at least they have one of their children within reach. Of course, young Hillary's marriage broke up—that was a shame. He seemed a nice young chap when he came down here that Christmas. Did you meet him?'

'Only once—at the wedding,' said Sara briskly. Before Betty could launch into further speculation, she said, 'Now, if you'll excuse me, I have work to do.' Rising to her feet, she opened the door.

Betty looked slightly disappointed. No doubt, she'd thought she'd been in for a good gossip session. 'Oh, right,' she said, standing and picking up her shopping bag and cardigan. 'Well, thank you, Sara—I mean, Dr Denton. It is nice to see you again.'

She paused in the doorway and, leaning conspiratorially towards Sara, added darkly, 'You do know you've got Desi Webster in the waiting-room, don't you?'

'Desi Webster?' Sara frowned. Not only was the name unfamiliar but she'd been under the impression that Betty Collins had been her last patient for that morning. 'I don't think I have anyone of that name with an appointment this morning.'

'Oh, he wouldn't have made an appointment.' Betty chuckled. 'Not our Desi—one brick short of a load he is, if you get my meaning. He just wanders in here when he thinks he will and he'll sit there until someone sees him.'

'I see. Well, thank you, Betty, for that particular piece of information. I think I'd better come through to Reception and see what's going on.'

Sara followed Betty down the corridor and saw the young man immediately. He was sitting in one corner of the waiting-room, playing with the toys they kept there to amuse children. Large, with heavy, thick-set features and dressed in baseball cap, T-shirt and jeans, at first glance he seemed just like any other teenager, but a close look revealed that he was, in fact, older than he appeared.

Sara approached the desk as Betty took herself off through the double entrance doors. 'Poli,' she said quietly, leaning over the desk, 'do we have someone else to be seen?'

'Yes, I'm afraid so, Dr Denton. We've adopted a policy when Desi Webster comes in.' Poli spoke in the same quiet tone as Sara so that the man in the corner wouldn't hear them.

'What's that?' Sara raised her eyebrows.

'Whichever doctor finishes surgery first sees Desi.'

'Who is he registered with?'

'He was on Dr Farrow's list—he hasn't been re-allocated yet.'

'And you're about to tell me that Dr Mason is still seeing patients.'

'How did you guess?' Poli pulled a rueful face.

'In that case, you'd better send Mr Webster to my room.'

'Very well. Thank you,' Poli replied. As Sara was turning to go back to her room Poli said, 'Oh, Doctor...'

'Yes, Poli?'

'He's quite harmless.'

'Good. I'm glad to hear it. But...' Sara paused. 'Is there anything I do need to know?'

'Well, here are his records.' Poli handed her the familiar brown envelope.

Sara glanced at the date of birth. 'Born in 1967. He's even older than I thought.'

'Yes,' Poli said, 'but his mental age is about eight.'

'All right. Thank you, Poli.' Sara turned and looked across the reception area. 'Desi,' she called.

The man looked up from the row of toy cars he was lining up along the edge of a table, his eyes narrowing as he focussed on her.

'Would you like to come in, Desi?' she said gently. 'I'll see you now.'

'Who are you?' Desi Webster ambled eagerly across the room, knocking over the cars as he did so and scattering them across the floor. He appeared to have no qualms about leaving them.

'I'm Dr Denton,' said Sara.

'What's your other name?' asked Desi, as he followed her to her room.

'It's Sara.' As she replied they were passing Alex's room. The door opened and Alex ushered a patient out.

'I like that name,' said Desi. 'Sara, that's a nice name.'

Briefly Sara allowed her gaze to meet Alex's, and just for a fraction of a second she swore she saw a smile hover around his lips. It was gone immediately, and he said, 'Hello, Desi.'

'Hello, Dr Alex—I'm seeing Dr Sara today.'

'So you are, Desi,' said Alex.

'I've hurt my leg,' Desi went on.

'Well, I'm sure Dr Sara will make it better for you.' Alex winked at Sara as she held open the door of her consulting-room for Desi.

'So, what have you done to your leg, Desi?' she asked a moment later, as he flopped heavily into a chair.

'I fell. I was climbing the wall and I fell. Look, it's all bruised and it was bleeding.' Breathing heavily, Desi rolled up one leg of his jeans to reveal a large grazed area on his shin, surrounded by purple bruising which was turning yellow at the edges.

'Oh, dear,' said Sara, examining it dutifully. 'Yes, you certainly did have a bad fall, didn't you? Why were you climbing the wall?'

'I was playing hide-and-seek—with the girls.' He flushed and grinned sheepishly.

'And did they find you?' asked Sara.

'Oh, yes,' Desi replied seriously. 'They found me when I fell. I yelled because I hurt myself so they knew where I was.'

'What happened then?'

'Julie went and got Mam. She washed my leg and put a plaster over the bleeding.'

'Well, I would say your mum did a very good job, Desi,' said Sara. 'It's healing up beautifully.'

'Are you going to give me anything else to go on it?' he asked anxiously.

'You know, Desi, I really don't think it needs anything else,' said Sara.

'OK.' Desi nodded and stood. 'I'll come back if it starts bleeding again,' he said. With that he turned, opened the door and ambled off happily down the corridor.

Sara watched him go, then picked up his records and began to read his medical history, which explained that, following a bacterial infection, he had suffered slight brain damage at birth.

'Did you cope?'

She looked up to find Alex, standing in the doorway. 'Of course,' she said lightly. 'He seems a very amiable sort of person.'

'Oh, he is,' said Alex. 'A bit too amiable sometimes perhaps, and the number of times he visits us can get quite irritating because nine times out of ten it's for something trivial...'

'But the tenth time it could be serious.'

'Quite.' Alex nodded. 'So we all tend to bear with the situation.'

'I see he lives up at Carter's Fields,' said Sara, glancing at the front of the envelope.

'Yes. He lives in a flat with his mother. I would imagine she sometimes has her work cut out with him because apparently at times he can be quite demanding. Apart from that, he seems harmless enough.' He paused and looked round her room. 'Have you finished?'

'Yes.' She nodded. 'I'm going to do a few house calls now.'

'What are you doing this evening?'

'Only taking Jason for a run.'

'Come over to the cottage,' he said casually. 'I'll cook supper—bring Jason with you if you like.'

She hesitated briefly, her first inclination being to refuse. But, then, she thought on reflection, why should she refuse? They both knew the score so there was no reason why they shouldn't be friends.

'All right.' She nodded. 'I will. Thanks, Alex. I'll see you later.' She really was doing rather well that day, she thought a little later as she left the surgery to start her house calls—first an invitation to lunch and then one to supper.

'So, how long have you lived in Longwood Chase?' Sara sipped her mineral water and appreciatively eyed the jacket potato which had just been brought to the table in the corner of the local pub.

'We came here four years ago,' Geraldine replied.

'We?' Sara raised her eyebrows before attacking her lunch.

'Yes, me and my husband, Calvin,' Geraldine replied.

Sara stopped eating and stared at Geraldine in surprise. 'I'm sorry,' she said slowly. 'I didn't realise you were married.'

'Actually, we're separated now,' Geraldine went on, 'but at the time we moved here we were very much together.'

'So, what happened? What went wrong?'

'Calvin was a rep for a computer firm. His work took

him away a lot.' She shrugged. 'The inevitable happened. He met someone else.'

'Oh, Geraldine, I am sorry,' said Sara. 'I had no idea.'

'Its OK.' Geraldine shrugged again, before biting into her baguette. 'I'm getting over it now, I guess, but at the time I really thought I was going mad. I wasn't sure who I hated most—Calvin or this other woman. I used to invent games where I actually plotted their deaths.' She shuddered. 'It was a very bad time for me.'

'I can imagine,' said Sara sympathetically. More positively, she added, 'But you've survived, haven't you?'

'Yes, and I think that was thanks to my job,' Geraldine replied. 'I started at the practice a few months before Calvin left, and I can honestly say I think it's been my salvation. It gave me a purpose in life. I had to get up each morning, I had to look smart and, because of the nature of the job, I had to have my wits about me. Dr Rossington and his wife have been especially good to me.'

'Yes, I'm sure they have,' said Sara. 'They are lovely people.' She paused. 'So, is your husband still with this other woman?'

Geraldine nodded. 'I sometimes wonder how he keeps up with her. She's a good bit younger than him. She probably wears him out. Still, serves him right.'

'It's sad isn't it, when a marriage breaks up?' Sara mused thoughtfully.

Geraldine nodded. 'I sometimes wonder now what it was all about—my marriage, I mean. It all seems such a waste—of time, energy, of life really.'

'Could you ever take him back?'

'Never.' Geraldine's reply was emphatic. She took a mouthful of orange juice.

'But what about you?' said Sara frowning. 'What about the rest of your life?'

'When Calvin left me,' Geraldine said slowly, 'I'll be honest with you, I thought my life was over. I felt old, ugly, unattractive... I thought no man would ever look at me again... But, well, things change...' She shrugged and Sara noticed a slight flush had touched her cheeks.

'Are you saying you've met someone else?' she asked curiously, feeling herself stiffen.

'Well, it's early days yet but, yes, there may be some-one...' Geraldine admitted.

'But that's marvellous. I'm really pleased for you,' said Sara. It was true she was pleased for Geraldine, very pleased, but once again she found herself wondering if the someone might be Alex. Not that it should make any difference to her even if it was but, all the same, for the briefest of moments she found herself wondering how she would cope and bracing herself as she fought a sudden pang of something very close to jealousy.

'Well, that's enough about me,' said Geraldine, break-ing into her thoughts. 'How about you?'

'Me?' said Sara quickly. 'What about me?'

'Well, is there a man in your life? I somehow can't believe there isn't.'

'Actually, there isn't.' She gave a short laugh. 'Not at the moment, that is.'

'So, are you saying there was?'

'Oh, yes,' Sara replied. 'There was. Very much so.'

'From the way you said that, I would guess it was serious.'

'Well, if you call living together for two years...'

'That's serious.' Geraldine paused, wiped her mouth with a paper serviette, then said, 'What went wrong? Another philanderer?'

'Oh, no,' Sara replied quickly. 'No, he...he wasn't like that. It was just that I don't think he was really ready to settle down, to take on the responsibilities of marriage and children...' She trailed off.

'And you were? Is that it?' asked Geraldine quietly.

'Yes. Yes, I was,' Sara replied. 'I wanted to be married and...and I wanted a baby...I really did. I thought that was what he wanted too, but I guess I was wrong.'

She was silent for a moment, wrestling with the strangest of emotions. When Geraldine made no further comment, as if she was waiting for Sara to elaborate further, she went on. 'He also made it quite plain that even if we did have children he expected me to give up my career, to stay at home and look after them. I wasn't sure I was prepared to do that. I've worked very hard to get where I am in my career.'

'Absolutely.' Geraldine sounded emphatic. 'So, what did you do?'

'I decided we were nowhere near as compatible as I'd once thought we were so I told him the relationship was over.'

'How did he take it?'

'I didn't stay around long enough to find out,' Sara replied. 'I went abroad to work. Unfortunately, that didn't work out either and I was forced to come home.'

'Have you seen him again—this man—since you came home?'

'Er...yes, I have, as a matter of fact.' It was on the tip of her tongue to tell Geraldine that it was Alex they were talking about, but something stopped her. Alex had said it was best not to tell because of the resulting gossip and speculation amongst the staff, and while she doubted that Geraldine would gossip she was still uncertain about the practice manager's own relationship with Alex.

'And how did you feel?' Geraldine was speaking again and Sara had to force herself to concentrate.

'I'm not sure really. Very mixed feelings, I suppose. I

was actually pleased to see him again. And I felt sad...yes, sad at the way things had turned out. I guess we should both have tried harder to sort things out.'

'Relationships can be hell, can't they?' said Geraldine.

'When they go wrong they can be, yes,' Sara agreed, pulling a face. Glancing at Geraldine and taking a deep breath she said, 'So what about this new man in your life—what's he like?'

'He's gorgeous,' said Geraldine, her cheeks turning pink again, 'but, like I say, it's very early days yet.'

'How early?' asked Sara lightly.

'I've only really seen him a couple of times, that's all.'

'Oh, *that* early.' Sara felt herself relax as her tension suddenly evaporated. If Geraldine had only seen this man a couple of times it could hardly be Alex she was talking about.

'Yes, but he seems keen so I'm really hopeful it might be going somewhere, but at the moment that's all I'm prepared to say. I don't want to tempt fate.'

'Do you think you and Calvin will divorce?'

A troubled look crossed Geraldine's face. 'I don't know,' she said. 'When he first left me he was desperate for a divorce so that he could marry this woman. At that time I was so hurt and incensed that I was determined I wouldn't make things easy for them so I refused.'

'And what about now?'

Geraldine shrugged. 'I must admit I'm seeing things a little differently now. Who knows?' she added. 'If things work out for me, I might just divorce Calvin.'

'It's strange how time changes things,' said Sara thoughtfully. She was relieved there was nothing between Geraldine and Alex. She wasn't exactly sure why she was relieved—she only knew she was. Glancing at her watch, she gave a sudden exclamation. 'Heavens,' she said, 'it's nearly two o'clock. I shall have to fly. I have an antenatal clinic this afternoon.'

In spite of her resolution to keep the whole thing casual, Sara found herself dressing with care that evening, before going over to the cottage for supper with Alex. She discarded several outfits, her bed becoming strewn with garments, before she settled on a sleeveless, ankle-length beige cotton dress with a design of black Egyptian hieroglyphics, which she teamed with a pair of flat gold sandals.

When she was finally ready she surveyed herself critically in the full-length mirror in Jean's and Francis's guest-room. With her short dark bob and tanned skin the overall effect looked exotic, a look she knew Alex liked. As she fastened a gold chain around her neck and added a pair of hoop earrings she wondered whom exactly she was attempting to please, but at the same time she found herself having to suppress a tingle of excitement at the thought of spending an evening with him.

It was a beautiful, mellow summer's evening and she walked the short distance to the cottage, with Jason padding dutifully at her side. She paused for a moment to watch the clear water in the stream beside the Old Mill as it bubbled its way over the bed of stones.

'You look stunning,' said Alex a few moments later when, in response to her knock at the door, he opened it and stood, looking at her, as she waited there on the step, a bottle of wine in her hands.

'You didn't need to bring that,' he said, as he stood aside for her to enter the tiny hallway. 'On the other hand...' he glanced at his watch '...I suppose it is "happy hour". Must keep up the traditions.'

Unable to cope with the look in his eyes, she lowered her gaze. The tradition to which he'd referred dated back to their time together when, on a Friday night, he would bring home a bottle of wine which they would share, after which they would invariably end up in the bedroom. The ensuing term of 'happy hour' had applied to that as much as to the wine.

'I was merely being the dutiful guest,' she murmured, setting the bottle on the dresser. 'And, in case you hadn't noticed, it isn't even Friday.'

'Need that make any difference?' he asked, then held up his hands. 'I'm sorry. I shouldn't have said that. I didn't mean to embarrass you.'

'It's all right, Alex. You haven't embarrassed me. I think we know each other too well for that.'

'Actually, while we're on the subject of apologies, I have another to make,' said Alex with a sheepish grin.

'Oh, and what is that?' Sara sat in the low rocking chair beside the dresser and looked up at Alex. He looked particularly handsome that evening in a dark blue shirt, open at the neck, and a pair of black Levis.

'I spun out my last consultation this morning,' he confessed.

She frowned. 'What do you mean?'

'I mean we went on to discuss village affairs, long after sorting out the man's health. You see, I happened to see Desi Webster come into Reception.'

'And you knew if you finished first the girls would ask you to see him…'

'Sorry!' He smiled and poured her a glass of wine from a bottle he'd already opened. 'Am I forgiven?'

'Well, I'll have to think about that.' Sara took the glass. 'Poor Desi, I don't know what all the fuss is about.'

'It's nothing to do with Desi personally—honestly, it isn't,' said Alex, picking up his own glass. 'It's more to do with the frequency of his visits.' He raised his glass and said, 'Well, here's to successful liaisons.'

'Successful liaisons?' said Sara warily.

'Yes.' Alex nodded. 'Purely within the partnership, of course.'

'Oh, I see. Well, yes, of course. I'll drink to that. There's nothing I'd like better than to see the partnership successfully established.' She sipped her wine and carefully set her glass down.

'So, does this indicate you may be thinking favourably about joining us?'

'It's still early days,' she replied cautiously.

'But are you enjoying working here?' Alex persisted.

'Actually, yes, I am,' Sara admitted. 'I've always loved Longwood Chase and, even taking into consideration the many changes that have taken place since I used to come here, I still like it.'

'What about the people?'

'They are interesting, mainly, I guess, because there's such a mixture of different types of folk.'

'And the staff?'

'Yes, they've all been very helpful.'

'And what about Geraldine?'

'Especially Geraldine,' Sara replied firmly. She threw him a quick glance and said, 'Why do you ask?'

'No reason, really.' He shrugged. 'It's just that at one time we had a few problems with Geraldine, but that was when she was going through a bad patch in her personal life. She could be rather prickly with the others.'

'I must admit I didn't know she was married...or, rather, I should say separated,' said Sara.

'She told you that?' Alex raised his eyebrows.

'Yes, we had lunch together today. She told me then.'

'She was devastated when her husband left her,' said Alex. 'And I have to say there are times even now when I doubt she's over it.'

'I sometimes wonder if one ever really gets over something like that,' said Sara.

'You don't have to tell me that,' said Alex softly.

Sara stared at him for a moment, then realised what she had just said and to what he was referring. 'Geraldine was married, Alex,' she said at last, taking a deep breath.

'I know.' He nodded. 'And I dare say there would be those who would argue that is vastly different from simply living together.'

'The commitment is different,' said Sara.

'Ah, yes, commitment—that word again.' Alex paused, apparently studying the wine in his glass.

'You were always wary of commitment, Alex,' she said quietly.

'Was I?' He paused. Then he gave a little shrug and said, 'Yes, I guess I was. I don't suppose I ever really got over the break-up of my own parents' marriage. At one time when I was in my teens I can remember thinking that I couldn't see the point of marriage at all if people were going to split up afterwards.'

'And now?' said Sara.

'Now?' He raised his eyebrows.

'Yes, what do you think now?'

'I think marriage should be for life, but I don't think the commitment should be made until both parties are absolutely sure it's what they want.'

In the silence that followed all that could be heard was the sound of birdsong through the open kitchen window. Sara felt a stab of misery as she wondered whether the reason Alex hadn't been able to make that all-important commitment had been because he hadn't been sure.

Desperately she sought for something to say, but at that moment there came the sound of a loud knock at the front door and they both jumped. With a muttered exclamation Alex set down his glass and went to answer the

door. From where Sara was sitting she could clearly see
into the hall, and as the door swung open she had a clear
view of the two uniformed police officers who stood on
the step.

'Dr Mason. Sorry to bother you. May we come in for
a moment?'

'Yes, of course.' Alex stood aside and as the officers,
a WPC and her male colleague, came into the cottage,
he turned and said, 'This is my colleague, Dr Denton,
who is acting locum for Dr Rossington.'

'Oh, yes,' said the male officer, nodding at Sara. 'You
saw my wife in the week, I believe.'

'How can I help you?' asked Alex.

'Well, Doctor, we have an unfortunate situation on our
hands.' The officer glanced from Alex to Sara then back
to Alex again. 'You see,' he went on, 'a child from the
village has gone missing.'

CHAPTER FIVE

'A CHILD?' Sara looked up quickly, her gaze meeting that of the WPC.

'Yes.' The police officer nodded. 'A little girl. She was last seen playing on the swings at the children's playground. We're making preliminary enquiries to establish who may have seen her.'

'Do you mean the playground on the recreation ground?' asked Alex.

'Yes, and the last person to have seen her says she was there at five o'clock. Her mother says she was due home at five-thirty for her tea. When she failed to return by six family members and friends searched for her but there's been no further sign. We were called at six-thirty.'

Sara glanced at her watch and saw that it was now seven twenty-five.

'Who is the child?' asked Alex.

'A girl by the name of Julie Jones. She lives on the Carter's Fields estate.'

'I know her,' said Alex. 'In fact, the family are patients of mine.'

The police officer nodded. 'That's one of the reasons we're here,' he said. 'To see whether you saw Julie this afternoon, and to ask if you will visit her mother. It appears the poor woman has become quite hysterical.'

'Well, I certainly can't recall seeing Julie today, but, then, I doubt I would have. I haven't been anywhere near the recreation ground. Come to that, I haven't even been up to Carter's Fields.' Alex paused, pushing his hair back from his forehead with one hand. 'In fact,' he went on,

'I can't really remember the last time I did see her. I'd have to check the records for that.'

'What about you, Dr Denton?' The officer turned to Sara.

'I'm sorry.' Sara shook her head. 'I'm afraid I can't help you. I'm new here and I don't even know the child. Like Dr Mason, I haven't been to Carter's Fields today, neither did I have occasion to go near the playground.'

'I'll certainly go up to visit Julie's mother,' said Alex. 'If I can be of any other assistance I'll be glad to help.'

'Thank you, Doctor,' the officer replied. 'A search is being organised at this moment and we may well be glad of further help.'

Alex showed the two police officers out of the cottage. When he returned to the kitchen he said, 'Sorry about this. Do you want to stay here, Sara?'

She shook her head and stood. 'No,' she said, 'I'd like to come with you. I may be able to help.'

'What about supper?' Alex glanced at the oven as he spoke.

'What were we having?'

'Chicken tikka.'

'Why not turn it right down to the lowest possible setting? Then we can eat it when we get back.'

'What about being on call?'

'We'll take the pager with us.'

Moments later they were in Alex's car, heading for Carter's Fields. On the way they passed several groups of anxious-looking people—some standing outside the front doors of their homes, others obviously preparing to join the search for the missing child.

'I don't suppose Longwood Chase has ever known anything like this before,' said Sara. 'It's usually such a sleepy little backwater.'

'I hope it doesn't have a tragic outcome,' said Alex grimly.

Sara bit her lip. 'Do you think it might?'

'Who knows with these situations? Usually if a child is safe they're found quickly. The longer it goes on...' He trailed off into silence.

'How well do you know the family?' asked Sara a few minutes later.

'Not particularly well. Just the usual—you know. Julie had chickenpox in the winter...'

'Is she the only child?'

'No, there's a younger one, a boy of about two. He's actually Julie's half-brother.'

'Second marriage, then?'

'No, they aren't married,' said Alex. 'Paul Thomas is Marilyn Jones's live-in boyfriend.'

Sara fell silent, closing her mind to possibilities. It was far too easy to find oneself jumping to conclusions.

There seemed to be even more people around than usual as they drove through the Carter's Fields estate, and as Alex brought the car to a halt in front of a row of identical houses the group around the gate turned to stare at them. As they got out of the car all muttering stopped.

'It's the doc,' said someone.

'Have they found her?' called someone else.

'Not as far as I know,' Alex replied.

'There's talk of dragging the river.'

'Maybe they should be looking closer to home,' said another voice from the back of the group.

Keeping her head down, Sara followed Alex up the path.

'Who's she?' someone asked as Alex rang the doorbell.

'Dunno,' another replied.

'His fancy bit, I expect.'

'No, she isn't.' This voice was quite indignant. 'That's Dr Denton. She's all right, she is.'

Half turning her head, Sara caught a brief glimpse of Grant Turvey's closely cropped head.

'Hiya, miss,' he called.

Mercifully there was only time for Sara to give a brief nod in reply before the front door was opened by a WPC.

They were shown into a living-room dominated by a television set and littered with children's toys and an assortment of clothes, drying on a plastic airer.

A youngish woman dressed in floral-patterned leggings and a large baggy T-shirt was sitting on the settee. She'd obviously thought the ring on the doorbell had heralded some sort of news of her missing daughter, and now that it had proved to be otherwise she was sobbing hysterically.

A young, thin-faced man was trying to control a very active toddler who had started to scream at the sight of yet more strangers.

'Sara.' Alex turned to her. 'Perhaps you could organise some tea for Marilyn while I talk to her.'

'Of course.' Sara looked at the young man, who muttered something unintelligible, before hoisting the toddler none too gently onto his hip and disappearing into the kitchen.

Slowly she followed him, leaving Alex sitting beside the sobbing woman on the settee and attempting to calm her down.

The kitchen was even more chaotic than the living-room, with the remains of a half-eaten meal of fish and chips on plates on the worktop amidst empty cartons and packets, tins, bottles and old newspapers. An Alsatian was tied up in one corner, and when Sara appeared it barked, snarled and strained at the rope that held him.

To Sara's relief the man opened the back door and released the dog into the yard. From somewhere beneath the debris he unearthed a kettle and crossed to the sink to fill it.

'Shall I hold him for you?' asked Sara, as the child began to struggle again.

'Yeah, all right.' Paul Thomas passed his son to Sara. The child's face puckered as he summoned a fresh scream, then he caught sight of the gold chain that Sara wore around her neck and began to play with it.

The man glanced over his shoulder as he stood at the sink, obviously surprised by the silence. 'He don't usually like anyone he don't know,' he said.

'How old is he?' asked Sara.

'Nearly two,' grunted Paul, as he plugged in the kettle and switched it on.

'And how old is Julie?'

'Seven,' Paul replied abruptly. While he rummaged about for mugs and teabags it gave Sara a chance to study him, unobserved. He looked a fair bit younger than Marilyn, six or seven years probably. His hair was long and straggly, he wore tattered jeans and a grubby T-shirt and there was at least two days' growth of stubble on his jaw. 'D'you think she'll be all right?' he said suddenly.

'I hope so, Paul,' Sara replied carefully.

'She's probably gone off with one of the other kids,' he muttered. He tried to sound casual but Sara noticed that a nerve was twitching uncontrollably at the side of his face. 'She does that. Marilyn's told her not to, but she still does it. Yeah, that's where she'll be—round one of their houses. Those Turvey boys, I expect. She were always hanging about with them. I used to tell her not to. So did her mother. They're trouble, that Turvey lot. Mouthy little sods an' all. But would she listen? That's more than likely where she'll be.'

Sara remained silent, not having the heart to say it seemed unlikely after three hours.

'I don't know how I'll cope with her...' Paul jerked his head in the direction of the living-room '...if anything's happened to the kid. She'll go mental—I know she will. And if anything *has* happened to her, I'll kill the bastard what's done it—I swear I will.'

'Paul, you mustn't talk like that,' Sara said, as the child in her arms began to whimper again. 'There's still a good chance that there's a perfectly simple explanation for where Julie is.'

'All right, then—what? You tell me!' He swung round on her, his eyes suddenly blazing.

'Well...' Sara swallowed. 'You just said yourself she may be at a friend's house.'

'That's stupid and you know it. I could tell by the look on your face when I said it you thought it was stupid.'

Helplessly she stared at him, uncertain just what she should say to this man. At that moment the kettle boiled and he turned away to pour the boiling water into a blue and white china teapot.

'I suppose,' she said after a moment, 'there's always a chance she may have wandered off somewhere and perhaps fallen asleep.'

'Or some pervert's lured her away—that's more likely so why don't you just come right out and say it?'

'That's a possibility, certainly,' said Sara, struggling to remain calm, 'but at this stage I don't think we should go jumping to any conclusions.'

'You see the news same as what I do. There's a kid goes missing nearly every week, and Julie's pretty... blonde...' His voice broke. He dashed his hand across his face to wipe his eyes, leaving a smear of grime down the side of his face. 'I wanted to go and help look for her, but the cops said to stay here with Marilyn...'

'I think that's probably best,' said Sara. 'Now, if that tea's brewed, how about taking some in for Marilyn? I'm sure she could do with one.'

They returned to the living-room to find that Alex had given Marilyn a light sedative, and that while they'd been in the kitchen Marilyn's mother had arrived.

'Hell. That's all we need!' muttered Paul. 'As if things weren't bad enough, without her showing up and poking her nose in where she isn't wanted.'

'I want her,' retorted Marilyn, 'so you can shut up!'

Marilyn's mother began to fuss, and attempted to take the child, whose name turned out to be Eden, from Sara's arms.

'Come to Granny,' she cooed, but the child began to scream again, coiling his arms tightly around Sara's neck.

'He's tired,' said Marilyn dully from the settee.

'Then maybe he should be in bed,' said Sara.

'Good idea,' said Marilyn's mother. 'You bring him up. I'll show you where the bedroom is.'

Sara glanced helplessly at Alex, fearing he might be ready to leave, but he nodded slightly so she followed the older woman out into the hall and up the stairs.

'This is a fine to-do, isn't it?' said the woman, as she pushed open one of the doors on the narrow landing.

'Yes, it is,' Sara agreed, following her into a bedroom which had a cot on one side and a small single bed on the other. There were several cuddly toys on the bed, together with a small pair of pink pyjamas which looked as if they were probably in the same place they'd been left that morning. Sara swallowed and found herself averting her gaze, unable to look at them.

'I can't even let myself think about what might have happened to that little mite.'

The woman's mouth began to work. Fearing she might be about to have another burst of hysterics on her hands,

Sara said quickly, 'Shall I put him down in the cot, Mrs...? Er, sorry, I didn't catch your name.'

'Call me Vi,' the woman replied. 'Everyone does. Yes, pop him in his cot. Worn out he is, little love. Here, let me give him his dummy. He'll go to sleep now.' As if to confirm her statement, the child's cries gradually ceased.

'I told her she was crazy.' Vi, still staring down into the cot, went on after a moment, 'At the time of the split-up I told her she was crazy. But would she listen?'

For one moment Sara thought she was still talking about her granddaughter, Julie, and it took her a moment to realise it was Marilyn to whom she was now referring.

'And when I found she'd taken up with this one...' Vi jerked her head in the direction of the door. 'I warned her at the time. He's a no-good, not a patch on Steve. Steve was her husband. I told her, this one would bring her nothing but trouble.' She lowered her voice almost to a whisper. 'And it looks like I was right...don't it?'

'Vi...I know this must be hard.' Sara stared at the woman and saw that her eyes were brimming with tears. 'But you mustn't start jumping to conclusions...'

'Can't help it, can I?' Vi sniffed. 'How can I help it when I've seen him clout her? And Julie...she's felt his fists and all. He's vicious, that's what he is. Steve may have had his faults but he weren't vicious. That's something he'd never have done...hit a woman or a child.'

'Where is he now—Steve?' asked Sara.

'Germany,' said Vi, with another loud sniff. 'Been working on building sites over there for over a year now. That's how the break-up happened. Steve were always away... Then she got trucked up with him.'

Sara looked down into the cot. 'Looks like he's dropped off now,' she said softly. The little boy's mouth still worked around the dummy but his eyes were closed, the damp lashes dark against his flushed cheek. 'We'd better go back downstairs.' She paused. 'Do you live locally, Vi?'

The woman shook her head. 'No, I live in London— Brixton. That's where we all came from before Marilyn was rehoused down here in this God-forsaken hole. Oh, no offence,' she said quickly, as she realised what she'd said. 'I'm sure you find it very nice, but, well…' She shrugged.

'You got here very quickly,' said Sara. 'Did they send for you?'

'Yes and no,' Vi replied. 'I'd been thinking of coming down, anyway. I'd had this feeling, you see, that things weren't quite right. Us mothers are like that. You got kids?'

She eyed Sara up and down as if she were looking at her for the first time. When Sara shook her head she sighed and said, 'I bet it's times like this make you glad you haven't. Well, like I say, I'd had it in my head to come down, then I get this call from Marilyn, saying that Julie hasn't come home. I told her not to worry, said that she'd turn up in a few minutes. Kids never have any sense of time, at least not when they're playing they don't.

'Anyway, at six o'clock she rang me back and said Julie still hadn't come home. By that time I'd already made up my mind and had my bag packed. I got straight in the car and drove down here.'

'Well, I'm sure Marilyn is glad to have you here,' said Sara, as they tiptoed out of the bedroom onto the landing and Vi pulled the bedroom door to behind them.

'She might be,' said Vi, pulling a face, 'but I doubt he is. He don't like me. He knows I had his number from the minute I set eyes on him—that's why he don't like me.'

'Even so,' said Sara, as she followed Vi down the stairs, 'I'm sure they'll be glad of all the support they can get at a time like this.'

'Are you Marilyn's doctor now?' asked Vi, as they reached the foot of the stairs.

Sara shook her head. 'Not exactly—Dr Mason is.' She nodded towards the living-room door. 'I'm only a locum at the moment, but for the same practice.'

As they entered the living-room Sara saw that Alex had been talking to Marilyn and Paul. Marilyn was still red-eyed but she appeared to be a little calmer than she had previously. The tranquilliser Alex had given her had obviously started to take effect.

Alex looked up, his gaze coming to rest on Sara. 'Is the child asleep?' he said. She nodded. 'Good,' he said. Standing up, he added, 'Dr Denton and I will go now but phone the emergency number if you need anything else. There'll be a doctor on night call and I'm on duty again in the morning.'

At the front door they stopped to speak to the police officer. 'Any news?' asked Alex. He spoke quietly so that the family in the living-room couldn't hear.

The officer shook his head. 'No,' he replied in the same low tones, 'nothing. Local places are still being searched—sheds, garages, barns and outbuildings. An appeal has gone out on local radio and television stations for householders to search their properties. If there's nothing after that, the team will start house-to-house enquiries.'

'Right,' said Sara. 'Well, you know where we are if you need us again.'

In silence they left the house. The group around the gate was even larger now, and there was a fresh buzz of speculation as the two doctors appeared. It gradually subsided as they got into Alex's car.

They remained silent as they drove away from Carter's Fields and down into the village again. It was Sara who finally broke the silence.

'It's almost impossible to believe what's happening,' she said at last, 'on such a beautiful evening as this. To think what horror could be lurking...' She trailed off, unable to continue. Turning her head, she looked at Alex.

His profile was set and grim. 'Do you think...?' she began. Then she rephrased what she'd been about to say and went on hesitantly, 'Could there still be a chance...that they'll find her unharmed?'

'Well, yes, of course. I suppose there's always a chance...' He hesitated, and from the tone of his voice she knew that he believed the chance to be a slim one, and one that decreased with every hour that passed.

'What did you make of the domestic situation?' he asked a little later as he drew up in front of the Mill Cottages and switched off the engine. Neither of them made any attempt to get out of the car, and Sara didn't answer immediately.

'I'm not sure,' she said at last. 'Marilyn was distraught, but that's what one would expect in those circumstances.'

'What about Paul Thomas?'

'Not a very pleasant character, I have to admit,' said Sara slowly. 'Marilyn's mother quite obviously didn't like him.'

'Did she tell you that?' Alex turned to look at her.

'Oh, yes.' Sara nodded. 'In fact, she didn't make any bones about that at all. Apparently, she wasn't happy when Marilyn split up with Julie's father, and when she got involved with Paul she told her she foresaw all kinds of trouble.'

'Any particular reason?'

'Well, I don't know about at the time—probably just

intuition—but since then she's apparently been proved right.'

'What do you mean?' Frowning, Alex threw her a quick glance.

'He uses his fists. She said she'd seen him hit the child, Julie, and I would guess that she'd seen evidence of his violence towards Marilyn.'

'Do you think she'll let the police know about this?'

'I'm not sure, although with what's happened now somehow I can't imagine Vi being backward in coming forward.'

Alex sighed and gripped the steering wheel so tightly that for a moment his knuckles gleamed white. 'It's so easy, though, isn't it, to prejudge a situation like this and simply jump to conclusions—conclusions that could turn out to be drastically wrong.'

He paused and in the distance they could both hear quite clearly the wailing of a police siren. 'Take the crowd around the house, for instance,' he continued as the sound receded. 'They'd only need to get a whiff of the possibility that Paul Thomas is responsible for Julie's disappearance and they'd be baying for his blood.'

In spite of the warmth of the evening, Sara shivered. Her flesh broke out in goose pimples at the image that this conjured up.

'Well, we can't do any more for the moment,' said Alex with another sigh, 'so I suggest we try to rescue the remains of our supper.'

'I'm sorry, Alex. It's delicious, it really is, but somehow I seem to have lost my appetite.'

Alex pushed his plate away, his own meal only half-eaten. 'Me, too,' he said. 'Have another glass of wine instead.'

Sara watched as he leaned forward and poured the wine, topping up what was already in her glass.

'It gets to you, doesn't it?' he said, as he topped up his own glass. 'Right here.' Putting the bottle down, he thumped his chest.

'I can't get Marilyn's face out of my mind,' said Sara. 'She must be going through hell. You simply can't imagine it, Alex. Supposing it was your own child—'

'Our child, you mean?' he said softly.

'Yes,' she whispered, her gaze meeting his. 'Oh, Alex, it's too awful.' Her voice broke.

With a muffled exclamation he rose and came swiftly round the table. He took her hands, raised her to her feet and folded his arms around her. He held her close, so close that she could hear his heartbeat, echoing her own.

They remained that way for a long time—a time of shared emotion as they faced the possibility of how they would cope if what was happening to Julie Jones's family had been happening to them.

For Sara it felt warm and safe within the circle of Alex's arms. With the rest of the world shut out, only the two of them existed.

Gradually, inevitably, other feelings began to intrude— a sense of familiarity, for they'd been here before, many many times, a closeness once born of love and then, quite naturally, steadily rising desire.

'Sara…' he whispered. 'Oh, my Sara, where have you been?' Slipping one hand under her chin, he raised her face to his so that she was forced to look into his eyes. That was her undoing. She'd never been able to look into Alex Mason's eyes, without being totally captivated.

A small voice somewhere deep inside urged caution and she knew this was madness. If she let this continue, everything she had sought to build in the last year—her freedom, her independence and that wall of immunity from Alex—would be destroyed.

She knew that so why did she let it continue? Why didn't she simply stop him when his other hand came up so that her face was now encircled in both his hands and the look in his eyes had utterly mesmerised her? Why did she allow his mouth to cover hers in a kiss reminiscent of thousands of others, a kiss that already stirred passions she'd despaired of ever feeling again.

Stop, Alex! Go away! Leave me alone. I don't want you in my life again, shrieked the voice of reason deep inside.

Oh, my love, how I've missed you, yearned for you, wanted you, whispered that other treacherous voice that tempted and urged her on to those unutterable heights of pleasure which, she knew only too well, lay in wait.

And it was the thought of that which rendered Sara helpless as she clung to Alex, the thought of that which led her to throw caution to the winds.

CHAPTER SIX

SARA was awakened by birdsong, and for a long time she lay very still, watching a shaft of early morning sunlight on the ceiling. It was too soon, too early for regret to have crept in. Time enough for that later. Besides, how could one regret something that had been so wonderful? Turning her head, she looked at the man who still slept by her side, and it felt so right that she should be there with him that it was as if the last year of separation had never been.

It had been like that through the night, with their lovemaking as natural and spontaneous as it had always been, followed by a sense of satisfaction that had left her satiated and utterly fulfilled. Alex had been both tender and passionate, and in that early morning light the only regret Sara allowed herself was that their love had had to end a year ago because their expectations had been so different.

That other regret, the one that niggled at the edges of her mind—the one that warned that now she could be back at square one—she refused to even contemplate further.

Even as these thoughts chased through her mind Alex opened his eyes and looked at her, and she was able to witness his first consciousness, his delight at finding her there in his bed.

'Sara...' he murmured sleepily, moving so that his body felt warm against hers.

'Alex, I...' she began, but he silenced her, drawing her

close and holding her against him, the feel of his bare skin delicious against her own.

'Don't say anything,' he murmured. 'I know it shouldn't have happened—that it was a one-off, and any-thing else you can think of to chuck at me—but I don't care because it was fantastic, every bit as good as it al-ways was. And because, I reckon, judging by your re-action, you enjoyed it as much…if not more than I did.'

The punch she threw at him landed on his upper arm and he twisted away. In retaliation, he rolled over so that his body covered hers.

'Alex…' she said warningly as she felt his growing arousal. 'We don't have time…'

'Why not?' His hand came up to cup her breast, and she knew it was only a matter of time before any flimsy defences she might offer would be down as he caressed her into submission.

'Because…because…well, there's Jason… He'll want to go out…'

'He hasn't made a sound. He'll be glad of the lie-in—he never gets a lie-in when Francis is around.'

'But…' Her excuses were sounding even more feeble. The shrill ringing of the telephone sounded suddenly throughout the cottage. 'Because of that…' she said.

'Ignore it,' said Alex.

'We can't. You're on call…'

'They can wait a few minutes, whoever they are,' mut-tered Alex with a scowl.

As the phone continued to ring there came a single, warning bark from Jason.

'It might be something about Julie…' said Sara.

'Yes, all right, I know.' With a deep sigh of resignation he moved reluctantly away from her and sat for a moment on the side of the bed while Sara, allowing her gaze to wander over his naked back, realised from the clamourings of her own body that she, too, bitterly regretted the intrusion of the telephone.

'I have to go,' he said a few moments later from the bedroom doorway. 'That was a call from a house in The Spinney. I also made a quick call to the police,' he added.

'Julie?' asked Sara quickly, and found herself holding her breath in painful anticipation as she waited for his reply.

'Still missing,' he said grimly.

'Oh, God, no. I thought—I hoped—she might have been found by now...that somehow she'd be safe.'

The spell was finally broken, the brief enchantment over, as the initial reason for their reunion—before passion had taken over—manifested itself once more and they were left facing the stark facts—a seven-year-old child had been missing all night.

While Alex speedily showered and threw on some clothes, Sara slipped on one of his shirts, then padded downstairs to the kitchen. Jason, who had slept on a rug under the kitchen table, rose stiffly to greet her, stretching each of his legs in turn while simultaneously wagging his tail.

'Hello, boy.' She bent and patted the dog's head and his glossy back flank, before opening the back door and letting him out. 'I'll take you for a run in a while,' she said, watching as he foraged around, exploring the unfamiliar cottage garden, 'but that'll have to do for the time being.'

Turning back, she filled the kettle, found the teapot and was just taking a carton of milk from the fridge when Alex clattered down the stairs.

'Kettle's on,' she said.

'No time,' he answered. 'I'll have a quick glass of orange juice.'

'OK.' Quickly she poured fruit juice into a glass and handed it to him, watching as he downed the contents.

'Must go,' he said. 'Sorry.' As he reached the door he stopped, as if the incongruousness of the situation had suddenly dawned on him. 'Please,' he said, 'help yourself. Make toast...coffee...anything. I shouldn't be too long.'

'No, Alex, it's all right.' She followed him to the front door. 'I'll have a quick cup of tea then I must get going. Jason needs a run and I need to change. I'll see you later at the surgery.'

'All right. Bye.' He kissed her on the cheek, then they both stopped and stared at each other. 'We're just like an old married couple,' he said with a chuckle. 'You, seeing me off to work at the front door of our cottage.'

'Quite,' she replied drily. 'The only differences being that it *is* your cottage, I'll be joining you later at work and...and we aren't married...'

'I know.' He hesitated on the doorstep. 'Sara, I...'

'Just go, Alex,' she said, turning him and pushing his shoulder.

'All right. All right, I'm going. We'll...we'll talk later.'

'Yes,' she said to herself, watching him as he got into his car, reversed and sped away with a wave of his hand, 'if you say so.' Going back inside the cottage, she shut the front door and leaned against it for a moment with her eyes closed.

They *would* have to talk later because now—because of last night—everything had changed yet again between them. No matter how much she might pretend that things could still be the same, she knew, deep in her heart, that everything had changed, and as yet she hadn't a clue how she was going to handle it.

She'd prided herself that she'd been coping.

Just.

Now, because of one night of madness, her emotions were in fragments again.

By the time she returned to the kitchen Jason was back and was sitting on the rug, cleaning himself. Mechanically, she gave him some biscuits then made herself tea. She carried the mug upstairs and set it on the bedside table beside the photograph of Alex's father while she showered and dressed.

Half an hour later, still in the same trance-like state, she let herself out of the cottage and, with Jason padding along beside her, began to walk back to Marshcombe House.

A light mist was lying across the meadows behind the mill but the sun was already warm on her shoulders and the air was filled with the scent of jasmine. It was hard to believe what was happening not far away, with uniformed police combing the countryside, on such a soft, fragrant summer's morning as this.

Sara was abruptly jolted from her reverie as a car suddenly drew up alongside her and squealed to a halt. She glanced sideways and saw Geraldine, winding down the car window.

'Hello, Sara,' she said. 'You're out bright and early.'

'Yes.' Sara swallowed. The last thing she wanted was for the practice manager to suspect where she'd been. 'Jason needs his early morning run,' she said, silently thanking her lucky stars that she'd taken the dog with her the night before. As it was, she feared that Geraldine was looking at the dress she was wearing and probably thinking it rather strange attire for early morning dog-walking. Goodness knew what she'd have made of it if Sara had been alone.

'Have you heard the news?' Mercifully, Geraldine seemed more concerned at that moment by current events, rather than anything Sara might have been doing. 'About Julie Jones?'

'Yes.' Sara nodded. 'It's dreadful, isn't it?'

'They've just said on the radio that the police resumed their search at first light and that door-to-door enquiries are going on. I don't like the sound of it. Anyway, I must get on. I'll see you in a while. I thought I'd go in early this morning. There'll be such a buzz with everything that's going on that no one will want to do any work.' With that Geraldine wound up her window and drove on, leaving Sara to complete the short distance to the Rossingtons' house.

An hour later she arrived at the surgery and wasn't surprised to find the whole place buzzing with speculation. Poli was wide-eyed, while Mavis, who had young grandchildren, was positively tearful.

'It goes to show what I've always said,' she said to Sara. 'Children simply aren't safe anywhere these days. Honestly, I ask you, if they can't play in safety at a children's playground then where can they play?'

'I know, Mavis,' Sara replied gently. 'It really is appalling, the things one hears about these days.'

There was also a restlessness among the patients that morning. Where on other days they might have sat in the waiting area without even looking at each other, today the most unlikely people were deep in conversation.

Sara felt quite strange, as if her emotions were on some sort of see-saw, with the events of the previous night producing both a high of ecstasy and a low of despair as she wondered what the future would bring. If that wasn't enough, the events surrounding Julie Jones's disappearance also evoked conflicting emotions, the surge of adrenalin that an event such as this inevitably produced coupled with a sense of dread over what the consequences might be.

In her consulting-room Sara flicked through the morning's mail, with its usual assortment of medical journals and advertising leaflets, together with the results of medical tests and X-rays, before switching on her computer. As a list of patients came up onto the screen she realised that instead of that morning's list, which she'd been expecting, the names facing her were those of the patients she'd seen the previous day.

Flicking the intercom switch, she waited for Poli's voice, and as she waited her eye ran idly down the list and came to rest on the last entry.

'Yes, Dr Denton?'

For a moment she was unable to answer Poli as she continued to stare at the last name on the list.

'Can I help, Dr Denton?'

'Oh. Oh, yes, Poli,' she said at last. 'I seem to have yesterday's list on my computer screen instead of today's.'

'You didn't close the file yesterday before you logged out,' said Poli.

'Oh, gosh, sorry,' said Sara. 'How silly of me. I'll never get the hang of these computers.'

'Don't worry,' said Poli. 'Just close the file now, then open the new one and you'll get today's list. I dare say you were getting worried, thinking you had Desi Webster for the second day running.'

After she'd changed the file she sank into her chair and gazed at the new list on the screen with unseeing eyes.

Desi Webster.

What was it he'd said? Something about climbing a wall and playing hide-and-seek with the girls. Yes, that was it. He'd been playing hide-and-seek with the girls. But what girls?

He'd hurt his leg when he'd fallen off the wall

and...yes. Oh, God, he'd said Julie had gone to get his mother. His precise words had been, 'Julie went and got Mam.'

She continued to stare at the screen. What girls had he meant? And Julie...Julie who? Could it have been Julie Jones? Could Desi really have been playing with children of Julie's age group?

'His mental age is about eight.' Who'd said that? Frantically, Sara searched her memory. Had it been Alex? No, not Alex. Then who? Poli? Yes, that was it. It had been Poli when she'd asked her to see Desi. 'He's quite harmless,' she'd said. Then, when Sara had commented that he was older than she'd thought, Poli had said, 'His mental age is about eight.'

If that was the case, surely it was quite feasible that he'd play with children? Maybe it was. Maybe he always had in the past. But things had changed. Things were different now. A child was missing. A little girl called Julie was missing and, by his own admission, Desi Webster had been playing with a girl called Julie.

Maybe she, Sara, was the only other person who knew that. Apart from Desi's mother, of course, and she knew because Julie had gone to fetch her when Desi had hurt his leg. But would she tell anyone? Would Desi's mother actually come forward and volunteer that sort of information under the circumstances?

Sara swallowed, realising to her dismay she felt slightly nauseous. Should she come forward and say what she knew? And if she did so would she be breaking patient confidentiality? On the other hand, what Desi had told her had only been said in passing and had hardly been of a confidential nature.

What if she kept quiet and Julie Jones was lying injured somewhere because of Desi Webster? Where did her professional duty lie? What did her conscience tell her to do?

Jumping to her feet, she crossed the room, tugged the door open and walked swiftly down the corridor to Alex's room. Hardly pausing to knock, she opened the door and swept inside. Luckily, he was alone.

'Alex,' she said, 'I'm so sorry to burst in on you like this...but I have to see you...now.'

His startled look turned to one of amused pleasure. 'Why, Sara,' he murmured, moving swiftly to close the door behind her, 'I didn't realise I'd had that much effect on you last night. I was hoping, but—'

'No, Alex, you don't understand. This is serious.'

'Oh, I'm being serious, believe me...so serious, in fact, I'm finding it rather difficult to concentrate on anything else this morning.'

'Alex, stop it. Please. You must listen. I simply don't know what to do. You must help me.'

Something of the urgency of her mood must have transmitted itself to Alex for he paused, and although the amused smile was still on his face he said, 'I think you'd better tell me what all this is about.'

'It's about Julie Jones,' she said.

The smile slowly faded from Alex's face. 'What about Julie?' he asked.

'Well, it's something I've just remembered. Something that Desi Webster told me yesterday.'

'Desi Webster? What's he got to do with it?' The smile had become a frown.

'When he came to see me in surgery,' Sara went on, 'Desi told me that he'd hurt his leg. He said he'd done it while playing hide-and-seek with the girls. Said he'd fallen off a wall.'

'Sounds like Desi,' remarked Alex.

'Yes, but that wasn't all,' said Sara. 'He went on to

say that when he hurt himself it was bleeding, and then he said, and I quote, ''Julie went and got Mam.'''

'Julie who?' Alex's frown grew deeper.

'That's the whole point. I don't know. It could have been anther Julie...' Helplessly, Sara trailed off.

'Or it could have been Julie Jones,' said Alex slowly. 'When was all this supposed to have happened?'

'Well, the graze on his leg looked as if it was a few days old.'

'So, even if it was Julie, it doesn't necessarily mean that Desi saw her yesterday.'

'No—' Sara began.

'But it could mean that they play together, and that Desi knew her well enough to ask her to fetch his mother.'

'Yes, but maybe that isn't so surprising. After all, they do all live on the same estate.'

They were silent for a moment, each considering the implications, then slowly Alex said, 'This injury he had. You say he said he got it when he fell off a wall?'

Sara nodded.

'What was it like?'

'Well, the skin was pretty badly grazed and there was bruising, the colour of which led me to believe it had happened a few days previously.'

'Hmm,' said Alex thoughtfully. Throwing her a quick glance, he said, 'Did you believe his story of falling off the wall?'

'Well, yes, I did. There was no reason not to.'

'And now?'

'Oh, Alex.' She threw up her hands in a helpless gesture. 'I don't know, really I don't.'

'Who do you think was chasing who in this game of hide-and-seek? Do you think Desi's injuries could have been from any other source?'

'What do you mean?' She stared at him.

'Well, for example, do you think they could have been caused by Desi being kicked?'

'Kicked?' Sara continued to stare at him. 'Well, I don't know. I hadn't really thought about it. He said he'd fallen off a wall…but, yes, I suppose the bruising could have been caused by him being kicked.'

'Do you think it could have been that Desi was being tormented by these other children? Kids can be cruel to someone like Desi, you know,' he added, when Sara didn't reply immediately.

'Yes, I know,' she said at last, biting her lip.

'You don't think there's a possibility there could have been some sort of incident the other day, which may have led to Desi retaliating or even seeking revenge?'

'Oh, Alex, I don't know.' She stared at him in dismay.

'Well, you're obviously bothered by this,' said Alex slowly, 'and you're not sure what, if anything, you should do about it. Isn't that so?'

She nodded miserably.

'All I'm doing is trying to make you see what the implications of this could be. On the other hand, it could, of course, be perfectly straightforward and exactly as Desi told you.' He paused and in the quiet of his consulting-room the only sounds to be heard were the faint hum from Reception and from outside the sound of children, playing.

'What you can't get away from,' Alex went on at last, 'is the fact that a child is still missing, a little girl called Julie, and that there are other children out there who also could quite possibly be at risk.'

'I'm going to the police,' said Sara abruptly.

'That's what I thought you'd say,' said Alex. 'If it's any consolation, that's exactly what I would do.'

* * *

In the end the police came to her at Marshcombe House during the lunch-hour, and Alex was with her. For that she was grateful. It was somehow very reassuring to have him there beside her, giving moral support.

'What's your opinion of this man?' asked the police officer, after Sara had told him the same facts she'd related earlier to Alex.

'Well, I hardly know him,' Sara replied. 'I've only seen him once.'

'From that one meeting, would you have thought him capable of abducting a child?'

'I really don't know...'

'Let's put it another way, then. What was your first impression of him?'

Sara thought for a moment. 'A likeable but immature man,' she replied at last. 'But, like I say, I hardly know him.' She threw Alex a quick glance.

'How about you, Dr Mason?' The officer looked at Alex.

'There's not actually a lot more I can add to that,' Alex replied. 'The family were patients of my late partner, Dr Farrow. They haven't as yet been re-allocated.'

'Is there any particular reason for that?' asked the police officer.

'How do you mean?' Alex frowned.

'Well, could the reason they haven't been re-allocated have anything to do with the fact that Desi Webster is considered a problem and there's a reluctance to take him on?'

'Not at all,' Alex replied emphatically. 'You'll find that many of Jim Farrow's patients have yet to be re-allocated. Those who have specifically asked for Dr Rossington or myself have been accommodated, but others who haven't expressed a preference are, for the time being, attending whoever is available.'

'Is there a reason for that?'

'Absolutely,' Alex replied firmly. 'We're in the process of taking on a third partner to replace Dr Farrow. That third partner will, in due course, take over the bulk of his list.'

'So what is your position, Dr Denton, in the Longwood Chase practice?' The officer turned his attention to Sara once more.

'I'm standing in for Dr Rossington, who's on leave in Canada,' she explained. 'Dr Rossington also happens to be my uncle.'

'Really?' The officer, whom Sara and Alex already knew wasn't a local man but one of a team who'd been drafted in to help cope with the crisis, looked surprised. He paused, looking from one to the other of them. 'Is there a chance you might be taking on this new partnership, Dr Denton?' he said at last.

'There is a possibility, yes,' Sara replied. 'A good possibility. The other partners have invited me to consider it.'

'I see. If you were to take up this position, would you have any qualms about taking Desi Webster onto your list?'

'No, of course not,' Sara replied. 'From what I know of him, I would say he's quite harmless...inadequate, maybe, but harmless.'

'Yet you thought it necessary to talk to us about your conversation with him. You obviously have fears...'

'I'm only relating what he said,' Sara replied. 'And that is that he'd been involved in a game of hide-and-seek with someone called Julie.'

'Can you tell us any more about his condition?'

'His condition?' Sara frowned.

'Yes,' the officer replied, 'the reason you consider him to be ''immature'' and ''inadequate''?'

Helplessly Sara looked at Alex, who then intervened. 'Desi Webster suffered a bacterial infection at birth,' he explained. 'That resulted in a slight degree of brain damage.'

'So what age would you put on his mental capacity?'

'No more than eight years,' Alex replied.

'Thank you, Dr Mason.' The officer stood.

'But that doesn't necessarily mean he could be capable of—'

'Of course not,' the officer interrupted, 'but I do think it necessitates a visit to the Webster household to have a chat with Desi.'

'I wish now I'd never said anything,' said Sara miserably as Alex returned to the Rossingtons' sitting-room, after showing the police officers out of the house.

'You had to,' Alex replied.

'Poor Desi, he'll be terrified when that lot turn up and start questioning him. I felt like I was in the dock myself—and I was only trying to help!'

'If he can't help them he's got nothing to worry about,' said Alex firmly.

'He'll still be scared,' said Sara, biting her lip. She felt terrible inside, and was beginning to wish she'd never thought of volunteering any information.

'His mother will be with him,' said Alex. 'Come on, Sara, cheer up. You had to say what you did. We can't lose sight of what's at stake here. Whether we like it or not, a little girl is missing. Whatever has happened to her, she, too, will have been scared, terrified even. Every possibility has to be explored—you know that. And if that involves a few people, including Desi Webster, suffering a bit of anxiety, it's a small price to pay.'

'Yes, I suppose you're right,' said Sara with a sigh. 'I needed to get it into perspective, that's all.' She stood up, walked to the window and stood for a moment, staring out at the summer splendour of the garden.

'I wonder what Jean and Francis will make of all this,' she said after a moment. 'No sooner do they turn their backs than all hell breaks loose in Longwood Chase.'

'They'll be concerned, certainly,' said Alex. Sara was aware that he'd crossed the room and was standing very close behind her. 'But at the same time I think they might be pleased at what else has happened.'

'What do you mean?' She stiffened slightly.

'Well, if your remarks to that police officer were anything to go by, it's beginning to sound as if you're well on the way to making the right decision about the partnership. I'd say that would really please the Rossingtons.' He paused. 'I dare say they might be pretty pleased by last night's event as well,' he murmured in her ear. 'I get the impression there's nothing they'd like better than to see us back together again.'

'Alex...' She turned her head and, in doing so, felt the touch of his lips against her cheek. 'About last night...'

'Yes?' he whispered. 'What about last night?'

'I'm not at all sure last night should have happened...' she began.

'You may well be right,' he said calmly. 'What we can't get away from is the fact that it did happen and, whether we like it or not, I think you have to agree that it was every bit as good as it ever was.' As he spoke he slipped his arms around her and held her closely against him. When she didn't answer he said, 'Don't you agree? Sara?'

'Yes,' she whispered helplessly at last. 'It was, Alex. Of course it was.'

CHAPTER SEVEN

SPECULATION was rife in and around Longwood Chase for the rest of the day, and by evening it had reached fever pitch. All police searching and questioning had drawn a blank and little Julie Jones was still missing.

'The thought that that poor little soul could be facing another night in the open...' Mavis shook her head in disbelief, leaving her sentence unfinished.

'I can't believe she's out in the open,' said Sandie Morgan, one of the practice nurses.

'Oh, dear, what do you think has happened to her?'

'Someone must have taken her,' Sandie replied. 'Either that or she's been attacked—'

'Don't!' said Mavis sharply. 'I can't even bear to think about it. Our Tracy's Jessica plays in that playground sometimes after school. If this was her I think I'd be demented by now...'

It was just before the last surgery of the day and some of the staff had congregated in Reception. Poli, who was sorting through records, looked up from the desk. 'Are you doing the extra surgery, Dr Denton?' she asked.

'For my sins, yes,' Sara replied. 'Dr Mason is taking the family-planning clinic.'

'I'm afraid you have quite a long list,' said Poli ruefully. 'This business in the village seems to have upset everyone.'

'In that case, I'd best get started,' Sara replied. Glancing into the waiting area, she added, 'Or, rather, I would if anyone was here.'

'I'll send the first one down as soon as they arrive,' said Poli, turning away to answer yet another phone call.

Sara made her way down the corridor to her room, and as she passed Alex's consulting-room the door suddenly opened and Geraldine came out. She looked pink and rather flustered, and hardly even acknowledged Sara as she hurried past her to her own room and shut the door firmly behind her.

Shrugging and then smiling to herself, Sara paused then retraced her steps. She tapped on Alex's door and popped her head round. 'I hope,' she said in mock severity, 'that you haven't been upsetting the staff, Dr Mason.'

He was standing with his back to her, looking out of the window, but at the sound of her voice he turned sharply. 'What do you mean?' he said with a frown.

'Geraldine,' said Sara. 'She came out of here looking quite flustered...' She laughed. 'What in the world did you do to her?' She expected Alex to make some witty quip or at least to laugh, but he didn't. Instead he, too, looked rather uncomfortable.

'I think everyone is jumpy and on edge at the moment,' he said at last, dismissing the incident.

It hardly explained what had happened, but Sara had the impression that the subject was now closed. As she went on to her own room it left her wondering if there might be another side to Alex that she had yet to experience—that of employer, in which he could prove to be a hard taskmaster. Briefly she wondered how he would be as a business partner and what she could expect in the workplace if she were to enter the partnership. She sat at her desk and stared at the bundle of patient records before her, wondering what he'd said to Geraldine to have made her appear so upset. At that moment the intercom suddenly sounded and she was jolted from her reverie.

'Dr Denton. Your first patient still hasn't arrived but we have a temporary resident here. Would you be prepared to see her now instead of at the end of surgery?'

'Yes, all right, Mavis. Send her in.'

'Thank you, Doctor—it's a Mrs Foster. She's just filling in her form.'

Sara had been prepared to see a stranger when her door opened so she was surprised when she looked up and recognised the woman who came into her room.

'Why, hello,' she said. 'It's Vi, isn't it?'

The woman nodded. 'Yes. Hello, Doctor. I was hoping it would be you I'd see.'

'Come on in,' said Sara. 'Take a seat.' She watched in silence as Marilyn Jones's mother came right into the room and sat down. She was wearing a loose blouse over a pair of cotton trousers and she looked tired and drawn, as if the strain of her granddaughter's disappearance was telling on her.

'Now,' said Sara kindly, suddenly feeling sorry for her, 'how can I help you?'

'I've done a stupid thing,' said Vi. 'I came away in such a rush I've left my tablets behind. They're for my blood pressure. I wasn't going to bother at first but then I thought that with all this going on I can imagine my blood pressure must be sky high.'

'Shall we just check it first?' said Sara, standing and taking the sphygmomanometer from the shelf behind her.

'How are you coping?' she asked a moment later, as she secured the cuff on Vi Foster's arm and slipped the stethoscope from around her own neck.

Vi gave a helpless sort of shrug. 'I don't know. I really don't,' she said. 'None of us have had a wink of sleep since it happened. Marilyn is just like a zombie, and as for that bloke of hers, well, he just gets more obnoxious by the minute. I don't know what the police are playing

at,' she went on after Sara had checked the reading.
'They don't seem to be getting anywhere at all.'

'I understand they've been carrying out door-to-door
enquiries,' said Sara.

'Yes.' Vi sighed. 'So I believe. Rumour has it on the
estate they've been talking to some chap who's a bit
loopy. Seems he used to hang about near the children's
playground...but I don't know.' She shook her head.
'Personally, I think—and this is just between ourselves,
Doctor.' She glanced over her shoulder as she spoke, and
when she was satisfied that the door was closed she went
on, 'I think they should be asking more questions closer
to home—you know what I mean, don't you?'

'Paul?' said Sara quietly.

Vi Foster nodded. 'I don't trust him—it's as simple as
that,' she said flatly. 'He's jealous of Steve and of the
relationship Marilyn had with him. Stands to reason he's
also jealous of Julie, doesn't it?'

'Your blood pressure's up, Vi,' Sara said, as she removed the cuff.

'It's no wonder, is it?' said Vi, with a snort.

'What medication do you normally take?'

'Propranolol—the 80 mg one. I take one twice a day.'

'Right.' Sara nodded. 'Well, I'll write up a prescription
to tide you over until you get home,' she said, reaching
for her prescription pad. There was silence in the room
while she checked the dosage and wrote the prescription.

'Do you think, Doctor,' said Vi at last, breaking the
silence, 'that I should tell the police what I think?'

Sara raised her head and looked at the woman. She
saw that in the time it had taken her to write the prescription Vi's eyes had filled with tears.

'What do *you* think you should do?' she said softly,
recognising the woman's dilemma as being familiar to
that of her own over Desi Webster.

The woman shook her head. 'I'm worried sick,' she whispered. 'I can't eat anything because of this knot in my stomach. Every time the phone rings or the doorbell goes it's a nightmare. God knows what Marilyn's going through.'

'So...?'

'I think I'd better tell them... Could I phone them from here, do you think?' she added anxiously. 'I don't want Paul to suspect anything.'

'Of course you can.' Sara nodded towards the telephone.

The police came to the surgery immediately. They questioned Vi Foster in the staffroom while Sara got on with her surgery.

No one seemed in any hurry to go home that night, and when all surgeries were over the staff congregated in Reception. Further searches of the countryside surrounding Longwood Chase were now under way, and although nothing directly was said it was pretty obvious to everyone that any hope of finding the little girl alive were now remote.

'Sara, are you happy to do the on-call this evening?' asked Alex, as he joined her in Reception.

'Yes, of course,' she said.

'Good, I've volunteered to join the searchers. If you have any problems before I get back, call Henry Jackson. He said he'd stand by.'

'Yes, all right.' She nodded and watched as, grim-faced, Alex left the building. Suddenly she had an over-whelming longing to go to him, call him back, embrace him, but she couldn't do any of those things. Whatever would the others think? Almost guiltily she glanced at the silent ring of faces.

'I can't bear much more of this,' said Poli, as the door

closed behind Alex. 'I've had a sick feeling inside nearly all day.'

'I know,' said Mavis. 'I'm the same. It's just too awful for words.'

'Well, I suggest you all get yourselves home,' said Geraldine in a voice that attempted to sound brisk but which, in reality, sounded far from convincing.

They'd all begun to disperse when the telephone on the desk suddenly rang. For a moment everyone stopped but no one attempted to answer it. The sound of a ringing telephone was as commonplace as breathing in the medical centre but, coming as it did at that particular moment, it seemed to hold a note of doom.

In the end it was Geraldine who took the call while everyone else waited in anticipation.

'Yes,' said Geraldine. 'I see.' She began to scribble on a pad on the desk. 'So, that's number forty-three. Right. Well, it won't be Dr Mason—he isn't here at the moment. No. It'll be Dr Denton. Yes. All right. Goodbye.' She replaced the receiver then looked up. 'That was a call from a neighbour of the Webster family. They want you to visit Joyce Webster, Sara. It seems Desi has been taken into the police station for further questioning, and Joyce has developed severe chest pain.'

'I'm on my way,' said Sara.

In direct contrast to the previous evening, with groups of people standing on every corner, the Carter's Fields estate was quiet, almost eerily so, its roads deserted and silent.

Sara drove slowly as she looked for number forty-three, following the directions Geraldine had given her. She wished Alex was with her.

She wondered where he was and pictured him as he tramped across open countryside, through ditches and woods and across streams, all the time searching for clues.

She shivered suddenly as if someone had walked over her grave.

A police car was parked outside Marilyn Jones's house, and as Sara drove by a quick glance revealed that the curtains were tightly drawn and there was no sign of any movement.

There was something unreal, even menacing, about the atmosphere so that by the time she reached the Websters' front door Sara was beginning to wish she was anywhere other than in this community that teetered on the edge of tragedy.

The two-bedroomed flat where Desi Webster lived with his widowed mother was in a block of four in the far corner of a cul-de-sac of similar, open-plan blocks, only a stone's throw from where Marilyn Jones lived.

As she parked the car and approached the house Sara felt as if the eyes of the entire neighbourhood watched her from behind net curtains.

Her knock was answered by a youngish woman who turned out to be the neighbour who'd phoned the surgery. 'I'm so glad you've come,' the woman said when she saw Sara. 'She's had quite a turn, I can tell you. She could hardly get breath at one point. It's not a lot better now either. Mind you, it's no wonder, with all that's going on.'

She lowered her voice, and with an uneasy glance over her shoulder she added, 'You should have seen the crowd outside here when they took Desi down to the station. Some of them were throwing things until the police stopped them. Desi was crying and carrying on and Joyce wanted to go with him but she couldn't because of the pain in her chest.'

'Did anyone go with him?' asked Sara, as she followed the woman into a small, airless living-room.

'The woman from the Social—that one with all those little plaits in her hair. It was her told me to ring you for Joyce.'

Joyce Webster, an obese lady of around sixty years of age, was half sitting and half lying on a two-seated settee in front of an enormous television set. Her breathing was laboured and erratic, her colour pale. One hand was pressed to her chest.

'Here's the doctor, Joyce,' said the neighbour, pushing the door right open.

'Hello, Mrs Webster,' said Sara, setting her case on top of a pile of magazines on the table. 'Could we have a window open in here, please?' she added, turning briefly to the neighbour who hovered uncertainly in the doorway. As the woman hurried to do as the doctor had asked, Sara drew up a hard-backed chair. She sat beside Joyce and proceeded to check her pulse, before quickly scanning the medication chart in her record envelope.

'I see you take glyceryl trinitrate tablets for your angina,' she said after a moment. 'When did you last have an attack?'

'A long time ago,' gasped Joyce. 'Haven't had one this bad before.'

'Do you have your tablets handy?' asked Sara.

'They're around somewhere.' Joyce looked vague as her eyes scanned the room.

'Never mind,' said Sara. 'We'll use a spray instead.' Opening her case, she took out a nitrolingual aerosol spray. 'It's the same thing,' she explained when Joyce looked suspicious. 'Open your mouth Mrs Webster, and we'll just put a couple of puffs under your tongue. That's right…just like that. You'll be amazed at how quickly it will work.'

While the medication began to take effect Sara glanced at her surroundings. There were the usual ornaments and knick-knacks which could be found in any home. On the sideboard were family photographs and on three walls pictures of landscapes, but the fourth wall, the one behind the door, was covered from floor to ceiling with large posters of Superman, Hercules, Batman and other children's cartoon and fantasy characters.

'They got too many for his bedroom,' said Joyce suddenly, and when Sara turned she saw that the other woman was watching her. 'He's got dozens in there. I didn't really want these in here but...' She shrugged. 'It's easier just to give in somehow.'

'What happens if you say no?' asked Sara quietly.

'He gets very upset...not violent, mind,' Joyce added quickly, 'just upset. Like a child, really. Only difference is you can reason with a child.'

'But you can't reason with Desi?'

'Not really. He doesn't understand, you see. He just sees a picture, he likes it and he can't see any reason why it shouldn't go where he wants it to go.'

'Maybe he has a point.'

'You know they've taken him in?'

'Yes, Mrs Webster. I know,' said Sara gently.

'For further questioning, they said. I told them he can't tell them any more than he already has. Desi doesn't lie—he doesn't know how to—but he was frightened, I can tell you that, even more so when he knew I wasn't going to be able to go with him.'

'I understand his social worker has gone with him,' said Sara, taking a fresh card from the record envelope and writing the date at the top.

Joyce nodded. 'Yes, Carmen. She's a nice girl and Desi likes her, but he'll still be afraid without me. It'll unsettle him for weeks and it'll be me that has to cope with him.' She gave a deep sigh. 'And it's all for nothing—he can't tell them anything.'

'I'm sure it's just routine questioning,' said Sara uneasily.

'If it's just routine why haven't they taken that lazy, no-good Barrie George from next door or Sid over the road?' For a moment there was bitterness in Joyce Webster's eyes. 'No, it's always Desi they want to blame when anything goes wrong, just because he's backward—that's all it is.'

'I'm sure that isn't the reason.' Sara had begun to write up her notes but she paused and looked at Joyce.

'Oh, what is the reason, then? You tell me that.'

'Well...' Sara hesitated, not wanting to be drawn into saying what Desi had told her or that it had been her who had spoken to the police. 'Maybe they just want to establish where Desi was when Julie disappeared so that...so that they can eliminate him from their enquiries,' she ended, resorting to the well-worn phrase.

Joyce Webster gave a deep sigh and then, to Sara's relief, she said, 'Yes, I suppose you might be right. They must know he plays with the kids—everyone knows it. I tried to stop him once—a long time ago when he was about twenty—but he got so miserable that, well, in the end I just gave up. I thought, where's the harm in it? He's just a child himself, really. It stands to reason he wants to play with other children... What else would he do?'

'Yes, Joyce,' said Sara gently. 'I'm sure you're right. But when something like this happens others tend only to see a child in a man's body and—'

'He wouldn't have hurt her,' Joyce interrupted. 'He's gentle, always has been. Neither would he interfere with her...'

'Joyce, you're getting all upset again,' said Sara. 'You must calm down.'

Joyce seemed to sag for a moment, then she leaned her head against the back of her chair and closed her eyes. Sara continued to write up her notes, the silence in the room broken only by the ticking of the clock on the mantelshelf and the faint sounds of Joyce's neighbour, who was presumably making tea in the kitchen.

'You know what I think?' asked Joyce at last.

'No.' Sara looked up and saw that Joyce had opened her eyes again. She seemed calmer, her colour was better and her breathing almost seemed to be back to normal. 'What do you think, Joyce?'

'I reckon the one they should be questioning is that Paul Thomas.'

'Oh?' said Sara. 'And why is that?'

'Nasty piece of work he is, and violent with it...not like my Desi. My Desi wouldn't hurt a fly.'

When she was satisfied that Joyce Webster's angina was under control and she'd checked her blood pressure, Sara told her to make an appointment to come to the surgery in a week's time. Then she gave her a prescription for further medication and, after a word with the neighbour to check that she could fetch the prescription for Joyce, she left the flat in the cul-de-sac.

It was still quiet outside, with the exception of a systematic thudding sound, coming from the side of the block. As she reached her car Sara automatically glanced back to see what the noise was.

Grant Turvey was kicking a football at the wall. When he saw her he kicked the ball into the next-door garden, where it lodged in the centre of a bush of lavender, then he sprinted across to her.

'Hello, miss,' he said. 'I thought that was your car.'

'Hello, Grant.' Sara paused, one hand on the doorhandle.

'You bin to see Mrs Webster?' Grant jerked his head towards the house. Luckily, it appeared to be a statement rather than a question and he carried on, obviously not requiring any sort of reply from Sara. 'They took Desi down to the station,' he added.

'So I understand.' Sara nodded and opened the door.

'Goodness knows why,' Grant went on. 'It weren't Desi she was talkin' to.'

Sara had been about to climb into the car, but she stopped and stared at Grant. The boy was kicking at the kerb with the toe of his trainers. 'What did you say, Grant?' she said.

'That day in the playground—it weren't Desi what Julie was talkin' to. It were some other bloke.'

Sara felt her heart give a painful lurch. 'Was it anyone you knew?' she asked quietly.

'Nah.' Grant wiped one hand across the back of his mouth. 'Weren't no one from around here.'

'Have you told anyone else this?' Sara leaned towards the boy but he didn't look up. 'Grant,' she said urgently, 'does anyone else know about this?'

He shook his head.

'But why? Why didn't you tell anyone?' She gazed at him in exasperation.

''Cos it was me what was playing with her before that. I thought they'd blame me. They generally do,' he added. 'Like they blame Desi for fings—only it weren't Desi neither.'

'You have to tell them, Grant,' said Sara, shutting the car door again behind her.

'Yeah, I know.' The boy nodded. 'I thought if I waited and told you, you might do it for me.'

Sara stared at him for a long moment, her exasperation

gradually turning to pity. Taking a deep breath, she said,
'Come on, Grant, let's go and find your mum first.'

'Thanks, miss.' The look he gave her was one of relief
and gratitude.

It was a good hour later before Sara eventually
drove home.

CHAPTER EIGHT

Sara had barely had time to feed Jason and put the kettle on for a badly needed cup of tea when she heard the sound of a car outside on the drive. Moving swiftly to the window, she was in time to see Alex climb from the car. He looked dishevelled and weary, and when she hurried to let him in he immediately answered the unspoken question in her eyes.

'No news,' he said wearily, pushing back his hair from his forehead. 'Nothing. Not a sign of her anywhere.'

He looked so tired, dejected and spent that Sara found herself spontaneously opening her arms to him.

Unhesitatingly, he moved forward and for a long moment they stood there in so close an embrace that she could hear the beating of his heart. Once again it felt right to be there. Safe, and utterly right.

'I'm shattered,' he admitted at last. 'I'm obviously not as fit as I thought I was.'

'Come and have some tea,' she said, moving away from him and leading the way into the kitchen. 'I was just about to have one. I've only just got in. I had a call-out.'

He sat down, exhausted, on one of the kitchen chairs and looked up at her.

'To Desi Webster's mother, would you believe?'

'His mother?' Alex frowned. 'What was that all about?'

'She had an angina attack,' Sara explained. 'They've taken Desi in for further questioning. No doubt the stress contributed to the attack.'

'Was she all right?'

Sara nodded as she filled the teapot and took two mugs out of the cupboard. 'Yes, I used a GTN spray and I've asked her to make an appointment for a week's time. She doesn't appear to have been seen by anyone for some time. I'd say she needs an assessment. For a start, she needs to lose some weight.'

Alex sighed. 'I've a feeling several of Jim Farrow's patients need chasing up,' he said. 'Maybe if you do decide to join us, Sara, that's the sort of thing we'll be able to get around to.'

Sara nodded, and as she poured the tea she said thoughtfully, 'Isn't it amazing, the knock-on effect of things in a small community such as this?'

'How do you mean?' Alex took the mug she handed to him, gratefully took a sip then settled more comfortably into his chair.

'Well, Julie Jones goes missing and Desi is taken in for questioning, which brings on an angina attack for his mother. I also had a visit from Julie's grandmother, Vi Foster, whose blood pressure is sky-high because she came away in a hurry and left her medication at home.'

'The stress can't be helping her either,' commented Alex grimly.

'I think it's beginning to get to everyone,' said Sara. 'And you haven't heard it all yet. There's been another development since you went out.'

'What's that?' Alex looked up sharply and stared at her.

'When I came out of the Websters' house,' said Sara, 'Grant Turvey was waiting for me.'

'And what did that little tyke want?' said Alex, pulling a face.

'Only to tell me that he was playing with Julie Jones

at the children's playground, and that Julie was talking
to someone when he left.'

'Who, for God's sake?' Alex lowered his mug and
stared at Sara in amazement.

'He said he didn't know who it was. A man, but no
one from around here,' he said. 'Which rules out Desi
Webster…'

'And presumably Paul Thomas as well,' said Alex
grimly. 'Whatever did you do?'

'Took him straight indoors to his mother and per-
suaded her to phone the police.'

'My God. I bet that was no easy task.' Alex looked
startled.

'You can say that again.' Sara pulled a face. 'Linda
Turvey never stops moaning at her kids, but let anyone
else as much as suggest they may be at any sort of
fault…'

'Quite,' said Alex grimly. 'Why hadn't he said anything before? Hadn't the police questioned him, for
heaven's sake?'

'Oh, yes. He'd lied to them. Said he was nowhere near
the playground that afternoon.'

'But why did he do that?' Alex frowned.

'I think the sheer scale of the whole operation frightened the life out of him. Apparently, he'd been playing
truant from school anyway and was in trouble for that,
and he thought if he owned up to being with Julie he'd
be blamed for her disappearance as well.'

'What's made him own up now?'

Sara took another mouthful of tea. 'I think he felt sorry
for Desi, seeing him hauled off to the police station like
that and then hearing that Mrs Webster had been taken
ill. I guess even the Turvey boys have a conscience over
some things.'

'So it sounds like the police could be looking for a stranger now,' said Alex slowly.

Sara nodded. 'What amazes me,' she said after a moment, 'is just how much we, as GPs, have been drawn into this whole thing. We seem to be a mixture of doctor, confidant and confessor all rolled into one. Goodness knows how poor Marilyn is coping with it all. We'll be getting another call to her next.'

They sat in silence as they drank their tea, each contemplating what else might happen. After a while Alex set down his mug and stared at Sara across the table.

'What is it?' she said at last, slowly lowering her own mug and staring back at him.

'We need to talk, Sara,' he said. 'Everything's changed between us.'

'I know,' she agreed. 'But...' She hesitated.

'Yes?' he prompted.

'I was going to say that, yes, I know we have to talk and I realise that because of last night everything is different but...but because of what's going on at the moment maybe it would be better to delay it until...until we know what's happened.'

'I think it's because of what's happening that I need to talk about it now,' said Alex slowly.

'What do you mean?' She looked at him curiously, noting the lines of fatigue on his face.

'I'm not sure I can explain,' he said. 'It was this afternoon when I was out there, searching—it was the strangest of times. We were searching so desperately yet at the same time we were dreading that we might find something. I can't describe how I felt. I only knew I wanted to put everything right between us. Those things that we argued about seem so insignificant beside something like this.

'I found I had to restrain myself from turning and running back to you. It was as if I had to check that you were still here, that something hadn't happened to you while my back was turned. If it had, I don't know what I'd have done... Am I making any sort of sense?' There was desperation in his eyes now.

'Yes, Alex,' she said, rising to her feet. 'You are making sense and I do know what you mean because while I was up there at Carter's Fields all I could think was that I wished you were with me. And then all I could see was a picture of you in my head as you were searching.' Swiftly she moved round the table and stood before him.

Wordlessly he put his arms around her and held her against him.

'Where do we go from here, Sara?' he said at last, his voice muffled against the folds of her skirt.

'I don't know, Alex,' she replied, as she held his head, her fingers running through his hair. 'I really don't. I think all we can do is to take one day at a time.'

Alex went home a little later, leaving Sara feeling exhausted from the events of the past few days.

'Will you be all right?' he asked just before he left.

She nodded. 'Yes, I'm going to take a bath then have an early night.' He looked up at her and the look in his eyes tore at her heart. 'We will talk, Alex,' she promised, 'but at the moment I think it would be quite beyond me.'

'I guess you're right.' He drove away, and she watched him disappear out of the drive before she turned back to the house.

In spite of her tiredness, sleep eluded her that night. She tossed and turned as snatches of conversation reverberated in her brain and images chased each other through her mind, forming and then fragmenting, only to reform like some demented giant kaleidoscope.

There was a child, a little girl with blonde hair, who laughed and danced at the edges of the picture. Sara had never seen Julie Jones but she wasn't in any doubt as to the identity of this dream child.

Later, someone was chasing her, this time someone with black hair plaited into dozens of tiny plaits, but when this person finally caught up with Sara it turned out to be Linda Turvey, who accused her of destroying Grant's football.

And, later still, she dreamed of Alex. He was standing in a sun-drenched meadow. In his hands was a pair of children's pink pyjamas and he was telling Sara that he didn't love her. That he'd never loved her. That she'd imagined it all.

She awoke, bathed in sweat and shaking, and for a long time lay listening to the dawn chorus and watching the bedroom gradually lighten. Was that what Alex had meant when he'd said that they needed to talk? To tell her that what had happened that night had been a mistake? That he didn't love her? That he'd never loved her? Did he want to make absolutely sure that she wasn't under any illusions about the future? After all, he'd actually confessed he was wary of commitment. He appeared to want her to stay but, if that was so, was he simply wanting to make certain that she knew the score? That if she did stay it would be simply as his professional partner?

Wasn't that what she'd wanted? It had certainly been what she'd said she'd wanted when it had first been proposed. Was it still what she wanted?

Could that one night of madness—because surely that was what it had been, summer madness—have led her to change her mind?

But it hadn't been only that one night which had churned up her feelings and, by his own admission, Alex's as well. It was something to do with the human drama that was unfolding in Longwood Chase—the high tension, the stress and the awful possibility of what might have already happened. All this, for them both, had seemed to contribute to a drawing closer together, to clutching at what they had to preserve and cherish it.

Suppose it was the opposite? Suppose Alex wanted to talk for a very different reason? What if he wanted to suggest they tried again? What then? What would her reaction be to that?

When she'd first come to Longwood Chase her answer would have been a resounding no. There would have been no way she would have been prepared to set herself up again, only to have to deal with the pain when it fell apart.

And now? How did she feel now? Was it any different?

Deep in her heart she knew it was different. Something had changed, although she wasn't sure she could actually put her finger on what that something was.

Restlessly she stirred, then sat up. Her bedside clock said it was six o'clock. She thought she may as well get up. There would be no more sleep now. Once again, as they had so often in the last few days, her thoughts turned to the missing child and she found herself wondering what the night might have yielded.

When Sara reached the medical centre it was to find that a police car was parked alongside Alex's Golf in the staff car park. That, however, had become so commonplace recently that she took little notice. It wasn't until she entered the building and found the receptionists in a huddle behind the desk and an electric atmosphere about the place that she realised something had happened.

'What is it?' She looked from Poli and Mavis to Geraldine. 'What's happened?'

'We're not sure.' It was Poli who answered. 'The police officers asked to speak to Dr Mason. They're in with him now.' As she spoke the intercom sounded and they all jumped.

It was Geraldine who answered it. 'Yes, Dr Mason?' she said. 'Yes, she's just arrived. Right, I'll do that.' She looked at Sara. 'He said would you go in, please.'

'Right.' Sara swallowed.

'Oh, God,' whispered Mavis. 'What do you think has happened?'

Without another word Sara walked down the corridor to Alex's room. She paused for a moment, bracing herself, before she knocked. As Alex's voice bade her to enter she took a deep breath then opened the door.

Alex was sitting at his desk and the officers, one male and one WPC, were sitting opposite him. They all looked up as Sara entered the room.

It was Alex who spoke, his eyes meeting hers. 'Sara,' he said quietly. 'Come in, please.'

'Is there news?' she asked, shutting the door behind her and glancing fearfully from one to the other.

'Yes, Dr Denton, there is,' said the officer. 'The child, Julie Jones, has been found.'

The silence that followed was so tense that for one dreadful moment Sara thought she might be about to pass out. It was Alex who came to her rescue.

'It's all right, Sara,' he said gently, sensing her distress.

'But...is she...is she...?' Wildly Sara met his gaze.

'She's alive,' said Alex.

'Alive!'

'Yes,' the police officer said with a nod. 'And, apparently, safe.'

'But where is she? Where was she found?' As Alex stood, Sara, afraid her legs were about to give way, sank thankfully onto a chair.

'She was found in Germany.'

'Germany! What in the world was she doing there?'

'She was with her father,' said the WPC. 'It seems—although at this moment it is, of course, unconfirmed—that she was abducted from the children's playground by her natural father, Stephen Jones, who smuggled her out of the country in his car.'

'Stephen Jones was told of his daughter's disappearance by the German police and, of course, he was questioned.' The other officer picked up the story and continued. 'But by then Julie was staying with friends of his and was being kept well hidden.'

'So how did they find her?' asked Alex.

'He came forward in the end,' said the WPC. 'It appears Julie was missing her mother so much.'

'And is she all right?' Sara was aware of an overwhelming sense of relief, a physical feeling so strong as to be almost painful as it flooded her entire body.

'We believe so,' the officer replied, 'but that's one of the reasons we're here. Julie is being reunited with her mother as we speak, but we want her to have a full medical examination. Could you go up there later this morning? We could arrange for a police surgeon, but under the circumstances we felt it would be better if it was her own local GP.'

'Yes, of course,' said Alex. 'I will be only too happy to go. Does anyone else know yet?'

'A press statement is being prepared now,' the officer replied.

'In that case,' said Alex, 'if you don't mind, maybe we could put my staff out of their misery.'

'Of course, Dr Mason. You have all been most helpful during this difficult time.'

While Alex saw the officers out of the building and spoke to the staff Sara remained where she was, sitting in Alex's room, as she struggled to get her emotions under control.

While he was gone all she could see was Marilyn Jones's face, and she could hardly begin to imagine what she must be feeling at this moment—to have imagined that your worst nightmare might have been about to be realised and then to learn that the hope you never lost sight of hadn't been in vain.

When Alex eventually returned the relief on his own face was now only too obvious. 'I doubt,' he said ruefully, 'we'll get too much work out of any of them this morning. It's going to take some time for the euphoria to wear off.' He paused, then moved in front of her and took her hands, drawing her to her feet. 'Are you all right?' he asked anxiously, looking into her eyes.

'Yes,' she whispered shakily. 'Yes, I think so. Oh, Alex, it's wonderful news.'

Slipping his arms around her, he held her close. 'It's more than any of us dared hope for.'

'I've never known anything to affect me quite so much as this has done,' Sara said after a while. 'Honestly, Alex, I call myself a doctor, but there have been moments in all this when I thought I might be in danger of falling apart. I can't explain it. I really don't know what was wrong with me.'

'Being a doctor doesn't mean we aren't human,' said Alex gently. He held her away from him as he spoke and looked into her eyes once more.

'I know, but I should be used to trauma by now.'

'This was a very different type of trauma. Not something, I must admit, that I want to come across again.'

'I think one of the things that amazed me with the whole thing was just how many people it affected,' said Sara slowly.

'Proverbial ripples in the pond,' said Alex. 'Reaching out from that one central point and touching people like Desi Webster and his mother and the Turveys.'

'What about Paul Thomas?' asked Sara.

'What about him?'

'Well, as far as I know, Vi Foster voiced her fears about him to the police. What do you think will happen?'

'That remains to be seen,' said Alex grimly, 'but I can imagine by now Social Services are well involved.'

'Alex, when you go up to the Joneses' house, can I come with you?' asked Sara.

'Of course you can. I was hoping you'd ask.' Bending his head, Alex gently brushed her lips with his own.

They went together after morning surgery. This time, with Alex at her side, Sara felt very different, even though the atmosphere at Carter's Fields was almost the opposite of that of the previous day.

There were groups of people around, just as there had been that first time, standing on corners, at garden gates and in doorways, but there the similarity ended. Today the air of relief was an almost tangible thing, and as Sara and Alex got out of the car a cheer went up.

The door at the Joneses' home was opened to them by Vi Foster, and even the policeman on duty at the premises had a broad grin on his face. Vi had little Eden in her arms, and when she caught sight of Sara and Alex she was too overcome even to speak. Instead, wordlessly, she led them into the living-room where Marilyn, her eyes almost black from lack of sleep, was sitting on the settee. By her side was a little girl with long blonde hair. Together they were looking at a book. They both looked up as Sara and Alex entered the room, and Sara was immediately struck by Julie's likeness to her mother.

'Hello, Marilyn,' said Alex. Crouching beside the child, he added, 'Hello, Julie—what's the book?'

Julie turned the book so that Alex could see, and Marilyn rose rather unsteadily to her feet. 'Is there anything wrong?' she asked, fear in the glance that flickered from Sara to Alex and then back to Alex again.

'No, of course not, Marilyn,' said Sara quickly, seeking to reassure her. 'Dr Mason just wants to check Julie over, that's all. You stay with them and I'll go and chat to your mum.' Leaving Alex to examine Julie, she went into the kitchen.

There was no sign of Paul Thomas or the dog, and the kitchen looked as if it had more than benefited from Vi's presence in the house.

'It's a happy day, Vi,' said Sara, watching as the older woman put her grandson into his chair and gave him a beaker of fruit juice.

'You can say that again.' Vi nodded. 'I was beginning to fear for Marilyn's sanity, I tell you. If it had gone on much longer I think she would have gone right round the bend. Of course, I'm getting the blame for it all now.'

'You?' Sara stared at her. 'Why?'

Vi sighed. 'Well, it seems Steve has told the police he took Julie because of something I'd written to him in a letter I enclosed with his birthday card. I told him I wasn't happy with the way Paul was treating Marilyn or the kids. Well, I think that was enough for Steve—red rag to a bull, really. He always doted on Julie, and I suppose he couldn't bear to think she might be suffering in any way.'

'As soon as I heard it was her father it explained why she'd gone off with him,' said Sara slowly. 'Marilyn seemed so certain she wouldn't have willingly gone with a stranger.'

'Well, he's in custody now for his trouble,' said Vi bitterly.

Sara glanced over her shoulder. 'Where's Paul?' she asked, lowering her voice.

'He's out. God know's where, and I can't say I'm bothered. In fact, I wouldn't care if he never came back.'

'And what about Marilyn?' asked Sara softly.

'Between you and me, I reckon she's frightened of him,' said Vi in the same low tones.

'If that's the case,' said Sara, bending to retrieve Eden's empty beaker from the floor where he'd thrown it, 'I should think, in time, she may come to thank you.'

'Well, we'll see.' Vi sniffed.

'How are you feeling?' asked Sara.

'OK, now I've got my tablets again,' Vi replied.

'How much longer do you think you'll stay?'

'Just as long as I'm needed,' said Vi, then added, 'Isn't that what mums are for?'

Sara and Alex left a little later. They were silent until they got back into the car, then Sara threw Alex a side-long glance. 'Well?' she said.

'She was all right.' He nodded. 'Apart from some areas of bruising,' he added after a moment.

Sara threw him another quick glance. 'Her father...?' she said.

Alex shook his head. 'No, it was old bruising.'

'So what happens now?'

'I put in a report.'

'What do you think will happen?' Sara frowned and, leaning forward, looked up at the house. 'Do you think they'll take the children into care?'

'I'm not sure,' Alex replied, 'but at least the authorities are now aware of the situation and the children will be on the at-risk register and carefully monitored, whatever happens.'

'What do you think will happen to Steve Jones?'

'Goodness knows. He did abduct Julie when all is said and done, even if she is his own child. Even if charges

aren't brought for that, he's wasted an awful lot of police
time and resources.'

'At least she's safe,' said Sara. 'And I guess, really,
that's all that matters. She's a lovely little girl,' she added
a moment later.

Alex nodded and switched on the ignition. 'I can almost understand Steve Jones, doing what he did. I dare
say I'd have been tempted to do the same thing myself
if that had been my daughter.'

Sara threw him another glance and saw that his jaw
had tightened. As the car drew away from the kerb she
said, 'Alex, do you think we could just call in to see the
Websters while we're up here?'

'Good idea.' He nodded. 'Now, what number are
they?'

'Forty-three. It's over in that cul-de-sac.' Sara pointed
down the road.

Joyce Webster opened the door to them and led the
way into the living-room where they found Desi slumped
on the floor in front of the television, watching a
Superman video.

'We thought we'd just call to see how you are,' said
Sara.

'I'm all right, thanks,' said Joyce. 'That spray you used
worked wonders.'

'I take it you've heard the news about Julie Jones?'
said Alex.

Joyce nodded. 'Yes, news travels like wildfire on this
estate.'

They all turned to look at Desi but he was still watching his video and hadn't even looked up when they'd
come into the room.

'Has he been all right?' asked Sara.

Joyce shrugged. 'It's upset him but, then, I knew it
would. Most of the time he's sullen and won't talk. When

he does talk he goes on and on about the police station. He'll be like this for weeks now. They've advised me not to let him go to the playground any more. Goodness knows what I'm going to do with him.'

'Isn't there some sort of therapy unit he could attend on a daily basis?' asked Sara.

'There's one in Petersfield. That's the nearest,' said Joyce. 'It was suggested once before but he refused to go.'

'Maybe it would be different now,' said Alex. 'Especially when he knows he's not to go to the playground.'

'Yes, maybe.' Joyce threw Desi a doubtful look.

'We'll try and sort out the details for you, Joyce,' said Sara. 'You must have some sort of respite care.'

'You up at the centre permanent now?' asked Joyce curiously as she followed them out to the front door.

'It looks as if I could be.' Sara smiled and glanced at Alex.

'Oh, yes.' Joyce, having intercepted the glance, was obviously drawing her own conclusions.

'No doubt that, too, will be over the estate like wild-fire,' said Sara as a few minutes later they drove away from Carter's Fields.

'I told you there was never a dull moment here, didn't I?' said Alex with a grin.

'You did. What I hadn't realised was that you'd meant it quite so literally.' Sara pulled a face.

'I must admit this last few days has been quite over the top, even by small community standards,' Alex remarked.

'I know. Francis and Jean are never going to believe it when they get back.'

They were silent for a while, but as Alex drove into the car park of the medical centre and switched off the engine he said, 'Did you mean it—what you said to Joyce Webster—about staying on permanently?'

'Do you want me to?' Sara allowed her gaze to meet his.

'You know I do,' he said softly. 'In fact, I'd say it's high time we had that talk. Don't you agree?'

'Absolutely,' she replied. She meant it because, although she didn't doubt that Alex wanted her to stay, what she did now need to know was in what capacity he expected that to be. Quite suddenly, that need had somehow become urgent.

In the end Alex came to Marshcombe House later that evening. He and Sara sat in the conservatory, watching the shadows lengthen in the garden as the sun slipped slowly out of sight.

'So you've decided to stay?' It was Alex who finally raised the subject.

'Yes, I have.' Sara nodded. 'It is a marvellous opportunity for me and I'd be a fool to let it slip through my fingers a second time.'

'Well, I'm delighted. I can't pretend otherwise, and I know Francis and Jean will be thrilled,' Alex replied. 'I'm sure it will all work out just fine.'

'I will, of course, be looking for that place of my own now,' she said carefully a moment later. 'I can't go on living here indefinitely.'

'I'm sure Jean and Francis don't mind.'

'No, I don't suppose they do,' she replied, 'but I'll feel I'm imposing if it goes on too long.'

'You can always move in with me.'

She allowed her gaze to meet his. 'What are you saying, Alex?'

'That I'd like you to give me another chance.'

At his words Sara felt her heart leap, but something deep inside still urged caution as she waited for him to give some indication that maybe this time the commitment would be greater.

'So?' he said eagerly. 'What do you say?'

She stared at him for a long moment then, taking a deep breath, she said, 'No, Alex, I won't move in with you.'

'Why?' he demanded softly. The look in his eyes was almost her undoing.

'Because,' she said, striving to keep her tone light, 'as you yourself said, your place is only really big enough for one.'

'Is that the only reason? Or are you trying to tell me there's no chance of anything further between us?'

She gave a little sigh. 'No, Alex, I'm not saying that…'

'What, then?' He was at his most charming, his most persuasive, as he leaned forward eagerly.

She continued swiftly, not allowing herself to become influenced by his charm, 'I don't want to rush anything.'

'I wouldn't have called that exactly rushing anything,' he protested mildly. 'After all, it isn't as if we don't know each other. We have lived together before.'

'Yes, I know, and it's for that reason that I want to take things very slowly this time. It didn't work out in the long term last time, Alex…'

'No…' he admitted grudgingly, 'but I—'

'I don't think either of us had really sorted out what we wanted out of life,' Sara said, not giving him chance to speak, 'and if we're not very careful now I think we could find ourselves in exactly the same situation again. To be honest with you, Alex, I don't think I could bear it if that were to happen again.'

He was silent for a long while, staring at the ground, then at last he looked up. 'What do you suggest we do?'

'I think we should go right back to the beginning and

start again,' she said slowly. 'Pretend we've just met, if you like—go out together, get to know each other all over again. Take it one step at a time and see where it leads us.'

'And you think that's really going to work?'

'Well, I think we could give it a good try.' She was silent for a moment, then she threw Alex a glance and said, 'What do you say?'

'It'll be strange,' he admitted, shaking his head, 'but, well, yes, I suppose it might work.' He grinned. 'I guess there'll have to be a few ground rules, though.'

'What do you mean?' Sara frowned.

'Well, for a start, do I get a goodnight kiss?'

'Of course...' She laughed.

'Oh, well, in that case we might as well go up to bed.'

'Alex Mason, you're impossible.' She sighed. 'That certainly wouldn't be taking one step at a time!'

'There was no harm in trying.' He stood and as she, too, got to her feet he drew her into his arms. 'I guess, in the meantime, I'll just have to be grateful for small mercies.'

As his mouth closed over hers Sara had to fight the urge to say that there was nothing she, too, would have liked better than to have gone up the stairs to bed and to have had him make love to her again. At the same time she knew that if she did, it would be only one short step from where they'd been before. And that was something she couldn't risk happening again. This time, if she were to live with Alex Mason it would be as his wife or not at all.

CHAPTER NINE

'HONESTLY, we turn our backs for five minutes and all hell breaks loose.' In amazement Francis Rossington stared across the table at Sara and Alex.

It was the end of the following week. Alex had collected Jean and Francis from Heathrow and had driven them back to Marshcombe House where they'd been greeted by an ecstatic Jason. Sara had prepared a meal for them all.

'You could say that.' Alex gave a rueful smile. 'But I have to say,' he added a moment later, 'that we coped with it all remarkably well, didn't we, Sara?'

Sara nodded. 'Yes, we did,' she said, 'although the experience of the missing child is not something I would wish to live through again.'

'It must have been dreadful,' said Jean.

'Yes.' Sara nodded. 'It *was*, quite dreadful. I still get nightmares where I see Marilyn Jones's face when she thought the worst had happened to Julie.'

'And you say it was the girl's natural father who'd taken her?' mused Francis.

'Yes.' It was Alex who replied. 'He was worried about her, apparently, and smuggled her out of the country.'

'What's happened since?' asked Jean.

'Well, he faces charges, of course,' Alex replied, 'though it isn't certain yet exactly what those charges will be.'

'And what about the other one—the mother's boy-friend?'

'He's facing charges as well,' said Alex. 'Of physically abusing Julie and assaulting Marilyn.'

'Is the little girl in care now?' asked Jean anxiously.

'No,' Sara said. 'There was no need in the end. Marilyn chucked Paul Thomas out so both children were able to stay with her.'

'Both children? Are there two?' Jean looked from Sara to Alex.

'Yes, there's a two-year-old boy,' Alex replied. 'He's actually Paul Thomas's son.'

'What a mess,' said Jean sadly.

'These situations usually are,' said Francis.

'It's the children I feel sorry for,' said Jean. 'They always seem to be the ones who suffer the most.'

'Jean is still suffering withdrawal symptoms from leaving the grandchildren,' said Francis. 'Aren't you, love?' he said kindly, with a quick glance at his wife.

Jean nodded. 'Yes,' she said. 'It was wonderful to see them again, but very hard to say goodbye.'

'So, have things died down now up at Carter's Fields?' asked Francis a moment later.

'More or less,' Alex replied. 'Would you believe, at one time young Desi Webster was getting the blame for Julie's disappearance?'

'I can imagine,' Francis replied grimly.

'Mob rule almost took over up there for a while,' Alex went on. 'It got pretty hairy, I can tell you.'

'I hope all this hasn't put you off joining us, my dear.' Francis turned to Sara.

'Well, I have to say I hadn't expected anything quite like that,' said Sara ruefully. 'Oh, it's true Alex had told me there was never a dull moment in village life, but I hadn't realised quite to what extent.'

'So it *has* put you off,' said Jean gloomily.

'On the contrary…' said Alex softly.

'You mean you're staying?' cried Jean.

Sara laughed and nodded as she looked towards Francis. 'Yes,' she said. 'If you still want me, that is.'

'My dear, of course we do.' Her uncle was on his feet. 'This is just the homecoming news I wanted, and I think it calls for a bottle of champagne by way of celebration.'

'What finally decided you?' asked Jean later, when she and Sara were clearing up in the kitchen, having left Francis and Alex deep in a discussion about general practice in Canada.

'I'm not sure, really.' Sara shrugged. 'It just somehow seemed right.'

'It wouldn't by any chance have anything to do with a certain situation?' Jean raised her eyebrows, the gesture both speculative and questioning.

'And what situation would that be?' asked Sara with feigned innocence as she began to stack the dishwasher.

'You know very well what situation I mean,' said Jean crisply. 'You can correct me if I'm wrong, but I'd be ready to wager that something has changed between you and Alex.'

'Well, you're right in one respect,' Sara began.

'I knew it,' said Jean with an air of satisfaction.

'But you needn't start listening for the sound of wedding bells.'

'No?' The disappointment on Jean's face was almost comical.

'Well, at least, not yet.'

'So there's a chance?'

'Maybe…eventually. I don't know, Jean.' Sara sighed. Leaning against the worktop, she looped her hair behind her ears. 'We had a long talk, Alex and I, after I'd decided I'd come into the partnership…'

'And?' said Jean.

'We'd already discovered we…we still have feelings

for each other,' she went on carefully, not wanting Jean to suspect they'd slept together again at the first opportunity. 'However, we both decided it would be wrong to rush back into something too quickly.'

When Jean remained silent Sara attempted to explain further. 'We felt…that if we did we might find ourselves with exactly the same problems that drove us apart before…so what we've decided is that we'll start from the beginning again and simply take things slowly.'

'You mean, like another courtship?' asked Jean.

'Yes, if you like.' Sara found herself smiling at the old-fashioned term.

'Well, I suppose that sounds all right…very romantic and all that,' said Jean dubiously.

'You don't think it will work?'

'I can't imagine Alex living like that for too long, especially in the circumstances…you know, where you've once lived together…'

'Well, we won't know if we don't give it a try. We'll just have to see. All I know, Jean, is that I can't risk rushing headlong back into something, only for it to all fall apart again. It damn near finished me off last time. I doubt I'd survive the experience a second time.'

'I don't think you'd find Alex would let you go a second time,' said Jean drily.

'Well, like I say…' Sara gave a helpless little gesture. 'We'll have to see. I'll be joining the partnership whatever happens.'

'That's wonderful. Your uncle is delighted, I know he is. It's what he always wanted,' said Jean. 'Your parents would be so proud of you if they were here today, darling.'

'I would never have got this far without you two,' said Sara huskily, fighting the lump that always seemed to come to her throat at any mention of her parents. 'You've been like a rock and I've always thought of this house as home.'

'Which, of course, it is and will continue to be as long as you want.'

Sara hesitated, then rapidly came to a decision and said, 'Actually, Jean, that is something else I was going to mention. Now that I know for sure that I'm going to be staying, I'll be looking for a place of my own.'

'There really isn't any need, you know,' Jean said. 'We love having you here.'

'I know you do, just as I love staying here, but my mind is made up—I'm going to go into town tomorrow to have a look around the estate agents.'

'I'm sorry, Dr Denton, but apart from Mill Cottages we don't have very much in the Longwood Chase area at the moment.' Sara watched as the young man in the estate agent's office thumbed through a folder of property brochures. 'Planning permission has been granted for a few more houses at The Spinney,' he went on after a moment, 'but they wouldn't be available until early next year. I take it you would be wanting something before then?'

'Yes, I would, really.' Sara nodded.

'You said you didn't want Mill Cottages, but can I suggest you go and have a look at it? From what you've told me, I'd say it might be just what you're looking for. Your colleague, Dr Mason, seems more than happy with his cottage. Look, why don't you take a brochure and give the matter some thought?'

Outside the office Sara stood on the pavement, reading the brochure. The cottage looked lovely and, as the young man had pointed out, there was nothing else on the market at present to suit her needs. If only it wasn't next door to Alex. She'd already told Alex it would be a disaster for them to live next door to each other, but that had been before. Before they'd reached this new understanding. Would it be such a disaster now? Maybe not.

On a sudden impulse she turned and went back into the office.

The young man beamed. 'Do you think we might be able to help you after all?' he said hopefully.

'Yes,' Sara said. 'On second thoughts, I think you might.'

A few days later Francis Rossington called a staff meeting at the Longwood Chase Medical Centre.

'The reason I've called you all together,' he said, when he had everyone's attention, 'is to tell you officially that Sara—Dr Denton—will formally be joining the partnership as a partner. I'm sure you'll join me in welcoming her. Sara...' Francis turned to her. 'Welcome to the Longwood Chase practice and we all hope you'll be very happy with us.'

There was surprised applause and delighted murmurs of agreement from the other members of staff assembled in the staffroom, and as Sara looked at the ring of faces she caught Alex's eye. He smiled and winked, and she looked away hastily.

'Thank you,' she said at last, when it seemed apparent they expected her to say something, 'thank you all. You've already made me feel welcome here and I look forward to a long and happy working relationship with you all.'

When the meeting was over Alex followed Sara out of the staffroom and down the corridor to her consulting-room.

'They're delighted,' he said softly, as he kicked the door shut behind him and spontaneously drew her into his arms. 'All of them—just as I knew they would be.'

'Alex,' she protested. 'Careful. Someone might come in.'

'I don't care,' he murmured cupping her face and briefly covering her mouth with his own.

'This is not what we agreed.' Firmly but laughingly she pushed him away.

'To hell with what we agreed,' he groaned. 'This is like some exquisite form of torture, being with you but not—'

'I know, but—'

A sudden knock came at the door, and they sprang apart like guilty children. 'Come in,' called Sara, pushing her hair back from her face and moving swiftly behind her desk.

The door opened and Geraldine came into the room. Without waiting for her to speak, Alex said, 'Well, this won't do. I must get on. I have house calls to do.' He nodded at Geraldine, before leaving the room.

In an effort to pull herself together Sara said, 'Were you looking for me, Geraldine?'

'Only to sign these letters, please.' Geraldine passed a wad of papers across the desk. 'And to collect your referrals.'

Thankful to have something to do, Sara began signing each one while Geraldine remained silent. It was only when she'd finished that she looked up and realised how strained Geraldine was looking. 'Are you all right?' she said.

'Not really.' Geraldine pulled a face.

'Want to talk about it?' asked Sara sympathetically.

Geraldine sighed. 'To tell you the truth, I don't know whether I'm on my head or my heels.'

'Is it work?'

'Actually, no. It's personal...' Geraldine hesitated,

then, with a little shrug, went on, 'My husband, Calvin, has turned up again.'

'What does he want?' asked Sara. 'A divorce?'

'No.' Geraldine pulled a face. 'Quite the opposite. He wants me to take him back.'

'What did you say?'

'I more or less told him to get lost,' said Geraldine bitterly. 'After all, what does he take me for?'

'What about this other woman he was with?'

'She's chucked him out, apparently. Honestly, Sara, he's the absolute limit. When he was with her all he wanted was for me to give him a divorce. Now she's had enough of him he thinks he can come crawling back to me. To make matters even worse, he's also lost his job. He looked really pathetic actually, but I guess that serves him right for what he put me through.'

'Where is he now?' asked Sara.

'He's got himself a bar job down at the Red Lion and he's living in. Says he's going to try and make me change my mind. I told him he's wasting his time.'

'Are you quite sure about that, Geraldine?'

'Yes, quite sure.' Geraldine hesitated again, toying with a pile of folders on Sara's desk. Then, as if coming to a decision, she said quickly, 'I told you before about this new man I'd met, didn't I?'

'Yes.' Sara nodded. 'You did.'

'Well, he's been very patient with me. He knows I was vulnerable after Calvin left, but I know he won't wait for ever so now I've decided I want to give it a try with him.' She picked up the folders. 'Is this all your referrals?'

'For the time being, yes.' Sara nodded. 'I'll have a few more later but I must get on with the baby clinic now.'

Geraldine walked to the door where she stopped with

one hand on the handle and looked back at Sara. 'How about you?' she said.

'What do you mean?' Sara looked up from the desk.

'Your man, the one you'd met up with again. Any further developments there?'

'There might be,' said Sara cautiously. 'We've decided to take things very slowly for the time being.'

'Don't take too long,' said Geraldine. 'I've come to the conclusion that opportunity doesn't knock twice—you have to grab it when it comes along.'

'Yes, maybe,' said Sara. 'We'll have to see.'

The baby clinic was always a riotous affair, with the doctor whose turn it was to take the clinic being joined by the midwife, the health visitor and one of the practice nurses. Even the receptionists were called upon to hold babies and care for toddlers.

There had been a recent spate of babies in and around Longwood Chase, and as Sara examined one after another she found herself once again swamped by the feelings of longing that had assailed her before. As a further reminder of those feelings, she found that her last patient of the afternoon was Mandy Richardson with baby Bethany.

'She's gaining weight,' said Mandy proudly, in reply to Sara's questions. 'And she's much more settled at night now.'

'You'll soon be thinking of returning to work at this rate,' Sara commented, as she picked up the baby from the couch and held her for a moment, cradled snugly in the crook of her arm instead of immediately returning her to her mother.

'Actually,' Mandy replied, 'to be honest with you, I'm not in any great hurry. I never thought I'd hear myself saying that—at one time my career was everything to me—but, well, it's all different now. I'm not sure I want to leave her.'

'I can believe that,' said Sara, as the baby's tiny hand curled around her finger, gripping it tightly.

'That business with the little girl who went missing really got to me,' said Mandy.

'I think it got to all of us, Mandy,' said Sara gently.

'I don't think I could bear to let Bethany out of my sight even for a minute.'

'You mustn't get things out of perspective, Mandy. What happened to Julie was a one-off.'

'I know,' Mandy replied. 'I do realise that, but it's made me look at what things are really important.'

'So, what do you think you'll do?'

'Well, I can't abandon my job completely,' said Mandy, 'and, besides, we need the money, what with the mortgage and everything. It wouldn't be fair on Duncan if I did that. But we've discussed it and I think I might be looking at part-time work instead of full time. At least that way I'll be getting the best of both worlds—keeping my hand in career-wise, helping with the family budget, but still spending time with Bethany.'

'That sounds a sensible sort of compromise,' said Sara, as almost reluctantly she handed Bethany back to Mandy.

'That's what it's all about, really,' said Mandy. 'Compromise and give and take.'

Sara watched her leave her consulting-room. Was that what she'd failed to do in the past? To see Alex's point of view? To compromise? To give and take? Or had it been Alex who had failed to do those things? Maybe neither of them had been ready to make those sorts of compromises before. Only time would tell whether or not anything had changed.

The buzzing of the intercom suddenly broke into her

thoughts. Sara sighed, leaned forward and flicked the switch.

'Dr Denton, there's an outside call for you—line three. A Mr Sharman.'

'Oh, thank you, Mavis.' Sara sat up straight, her concentration restored. 'Put him through, please. Mr Sharman?'

'Hello, Dr Denton. Just thought you'd like to know that I have the keys to number two, Mill Cottages. I could arrange a time for you to come with me to see the cottage. Alternatively, I shall be passing through Longwood Chase on my way home from work and I could drop the keys into the surgery. As you know, the cottage is empty so you could then go and see it at your leisure.'

'That would be great. Thank you, Mr Sharman. Thank you very much.' With a smile Sara replaced the receiver.

Suddenly she wanted to tell Alex, wanted to see his face, maybe go home with him so they could look at the cottage together. However, by the time Mr Sharman had delivered the keys and it was time for her to leave the surgery Alex was still out on house calls so she decided to walk down to Mill Cottages on her own.

It had rained during the day but the clouds had dispersed towards evening, leaving that wonderful green freshness so typical of an English summer's day. The grass around the mill stream was thick with celandine and wild musk, while the gardens of the cottages were a mass of colour.

Sara paused for a moment to inspect the shrubs and flowers in front of number two. She knew little about plants or gardening, but as she fitted the key in the lock she decided that if she did buy the cottage it would be something she'd have to learn in order to keep the garden looking as colourful and attractive as it did at present.

The smell of fresh paint hit Sara as the door swung

open and she stepped straight into the living room. The layout of the cottage was the same as Alex's but reversed.

Slowly, but with a growing sense of excitement that all this could soon be hers, Sara wandered from the living-room to the kitchen then up the narrow staircase to the two tiny bedrooms above.

One of the bedrooms overlooked the mill stream while the other, the smaller of the two, looked out over fields and farmland to the distant line of the downs. It was while she was standing there, admiring the view, that she heard a sound downstairs. She turned from the window as a voice called out from below.

'Hello, there.'

Smiling to herself, she walked to the top of the stairs and looked over the bannister. Alex was standing at the foot of the stairs, gazing up at her in astonishment.

'Sara!' he said. 'I heard a noise in here. I thought it was burglars or, failing that, squatters.'

'No, nothing like that. Just a prospective buyer, that's all.'

He stared at her in amazement. 'You mean…?'

'Yes, Alex, number two, Mill Cottages could soon be mine.'

'But that's wonderful!' He continued to stare at her as if he still couldn't quite believe it as she came down the stairs and stood beside him. 'When we spoke of it before you sounded as if it would be the last place on earth you'd want to buy.'

'That was then,' said Sara lightly. 'Things are different now.'

'Different?'

'Well, everything has changed now, hasn't it?' she said, looking up into his face.

'Tell me.' There was amusement in his eyes now. 'I want to hear you say what things have changed.'

'For a start, I'm now a permanent resident of Longwood Chase...'

'Go on...'

'And a partner at the surgery...'

'And?'

'Is there more?'

'Isn't the fact that we made love again a significant factor?'

'Oh, yes, there's that,' she said. 'Silly me. I hadn't given that a thought...'

Roughly he pulled her into his arms and his mouth crushed hers, silencing anything else she might have been about to say.

'Maybe,' he said at last, between kisses, 'I need to be a little more thorough. Make sure you don't forget.' Urgently his hands roamed over her body until at last she pulled away from him, laughing.

'I also seem to remember the other thing that happened was that we agreed to start again...'

'Isn't that what we're doing?' he protested with a groan.

'That we'd take things very slowly,' she said with mock severity. 'One step at a time, we said.'

'All right. Point taken. I'm sorry. I'll behave. I promise.' He stepped away from her. 'But, if that's to be,' he added, 'I need something to take my mind off it.'

'Right. Come on, let me show you round the cottage.'

'You're on. Lead the way.' With a flourish he stepped aside, allowing her to precede him into the kitchen.

'There's not really very much room,' she said a moment later as she gazed around the tiny room with its old-fashioned fixtures. ·

'But, as you once pointed out to me, there's plenty of room for one,' said Alex. 'Mind you, if that wall through there in the living-room were knocked down, it would make a vast difference.'

'But what's on the other side?' Sara looked bewildered.

'My living-room,' said Alex seriously.

'Your living-room...?' said Sara.

'Yes,' said Alex, leaning forward and kissing the tip of her nose, 'my living room. So when you finally decide you're ready to live with me again all we'll have to do is to get it knocked down.'

CHAPTER TEN

SLOWLY Sara sank onto the bed, still staring at the small plastic object in her hand. Could she be mistaken? Was she seeing something that wasn't there? No, there was no mistaking the presence of the thin, but definite, blue line.

She was pregnant.

Her first and immediate reaction after the initial shock was one of overwhelming joy. She was going to have a baby. Alex's baby. Even now the crucial cells were dividing inside her body and had been doing so since that night they'd spent together—cells that determined gender, that carried the genes that decided on blue eyes or brown, straight hair or curly.

Images of babies flooded her mind—babies like Bethany whose tiny hand had curled round her finger, like little Eden who had snuggled into her arms, like all those other babies she handled every week in the baby clinic and who had been indirectly responsible for the ache of longing which had been steadily growing in her heart. And now that ache was about to be satisfied. She, too, was to be a mother... She—

'Sara!'

She was brought back to earth abruptly by the sound of Jean's voice from downstairs.

'Do you know the time?'

'Yes,' she called back. 'I'm just coming.'

She was late and she knew it. It was the first time she'd ever been late for surgery but somehow it didn't matter. Even when she received strange looks from Poli and

Mavis when—eventually—she did arrive at the centre she hardly noticed because she felt as if she were walking on air.

Because she was so late there was no sign of Alex, who'd already started his own surgery. Strangely, she found herself grateful for that because while part of her longed to see him another part of her was dreading it. Already memories of that other time had begun to creep back—the time when she'd thought she might have been pregnant and Alex had been less than pleased.

She managed to pull herself together sufficiently to see the first of the patients on that morning's list, but after only half an hour she stopped and went to the staffroom to pour herself a coffee. Curling her hands—which felt surprisingly cold for the time of the year—around the mug, she wandered to the window and stared out.

Small children were playing in the playground of the primary school next door—little girls in gingham dresses and small boys their hair cut in trendy, fashionable styles. Motherhood wasn't only about smiles and cuddles and joy—it was about anxiety and responsibility. It was about the anguish of Marilyn Jones, the frustration and help-lessness of Joyce Webster and the numbing tiredness of Mandy Richardson. It was about total commitment and the unseen bonds of love that bound families together.

She took a gulp of her coffee and in a moment of blind panic abruptly turned away from the window.

Could she have made a mistake? Had the test been wrong? After all, it had only been that one night and they had taken precautions...at least, they had to start with, but what about later in the middle of the night when Alex had reached out for her again and again? She couldn't remember. She really couldn't.

Ten minutes later she was staring at a thin blue line once more. There was no mistake. In the past women had

had to wait until a second period had been missed before they'd been sure. Today things were different. Women knew immediately, which really was how it should be, Sara thought as she washed her hands and prepared to resume her surgery. After all, you were either pregnant or you weren't. The condition was determined at the moment of conception, not at some elusive point in the following weeks.

Euphoria surged again and it wasn't until nearly lunchtime that reality began to creep in and she started to face the practicalities of her situation.

Really, it couldn't have happened at a more difficult time. For a start, she and Alex weren't married—weren't even in a long-term relationship any more. Neither had there been anything to lead Sara to believe that if they did get together again it would be any different from the last time. It had been she who'd insisted that they started again from the beginning, that they took this new relationship slowly. Now she was pregnant, one of the issues which had caused difficulties the last time they'd been together.

Alex hadn't been keen on the idea of starting a family, at least not for some considerable time, and their final arguments had been over whether or not—if she *had* been pregnant—she would have put her career on hold to have a family or carried on working...

'Dr Denton, are you all right?'

Sara looked up sharply to find Poli in front of her desk, looking down at her in concern. She'd been so lost in her thoughts that she hadn't even heard the receptionist come into the room.

'Oh, yes. Yes, Poli,' she said at last, 'I'm fine.'

'You don't look fine,' said Poli dubiously.

'I am, really, I am.' Hastily she looped her hair behind her ears. 'Are there any more patients, Poli?'

'No, that's the last. You have a couple of house calls, though.'

'Thanks. Oh, Poli,' she said, as the girl turned to leave, 'Is Dr Mason in his room?'

'No, he's already left to do his house calls. Dr Rossington is still here, I believe. He said something about a partnership meeting after lunch.'

The partnership. Sara stared in dismay at the closed door as Poli went back to Reception. She'd forgotten all about the partnership.

What on earth would her uncle say when he knew she was pregnant? She'd only just signed the contract, for heaven's sake. She couldn't imagine his reaction when she started talking about maternity leave.

And then there was the cottage. What of that? She'd only just completed the mortgage application—would she still be able to meet the payments? Of course she would—after all, her salary would be the same when she returned after maternity leave.

But, a little voice niggled inside her head, Alex had said he didn't want his children looked after by strangers. At the time she'd thought him old-fashioned and out of touch, but now, how did she feel about that now?

Would she want to leave her baby, any more than Mandy Richardson wanted to leave Bethany? She, too, had wanted to go straight back to work at the first opportunity—until she'd been faced with the reality of the situation.

With a little groan Sara put her arms on the desk and rested her head on them. She was still like that a few moments later when Geraldine tapped on the door and looked into the room.

'Sara, what is it?' She came right inside then and closed the door behind her. 'Poli said she thought there was something wrong. What is it? Can I help?'

With a deep sigh Sara lifted her head. 'No, Geraldine,' she said at last. 'There isn't anything you can do. In fact, I doubt there's anything anyone can do.'

'Try me,' said Geraldine. 'I might not be able to fix it, but I'm a good listener.'

Sara stared at her. Maybe it would be good to talk to someone. Maybe another woman would help her to get her chaotic thoughts into some sort of order.

'It wouldn't go any further,' said Geraldine. 'Confidentiality is my middle name. Let's face it, as practice manager it has to be. Not only do I know things about the patients, I end up being a mother-figure to the staff as well—and, more often than not, that includes the doctors.'

'I'm pregnant,' said Sara bluntly.

'Phew!' Geraldine stared at her. 'Well, that's a first, I must say...and a surprise,' she admitted at last.

'Yes, it surprised me too,' said Sara wryly.

'Are you certain?'

'Oh, yes. I've done two tests.'

'Right. Well, from your reaction, I gather it wasn't planned. Next step—do you want to keep it?'

'What?' Sara stared blankly at Geraldine.

'Is termination an option?'

'No.' Her reply was instant. 'No...I want it.'

'Fair enough. In that case,' Geraldine went on calmly, 'does the father know?'

Sara slowly shook her head. 'No,' she said at last. 'I've only just found out myself.'

'How reliable are the tests? Could they be wrong?'

Sara shook her head again. 'They're not wrong,' she said. 'I know they're not wrong.'

'OK.' Geraldine sat on the chair opposite Sara, and leaning forward, rested her elbows on the desk. 'So, the father. Is it the man you were telling me about? The man that has come back into your life again?'

'Yes.' Sara nodded. 'Yes, it's him.' Somehow she now found it even more impossible to tell Geraldine it was Alex they were talking about.

'How do you think he'll react when you tell him?'

'Heaven only knows!'

'You said when you were with this man before that you lived together for some time—had you discussed marriage?'

'Oh, yes.' Sara sighed. 'Yes, we had—but I guess it wasn't the right time.'

'Maybe now is the right time,' said Geraldine gently. 'Now that there's a baby on the way.'

'I don't know.' Sara shook her head. 'I really don't know, Geraldine.' She paused. 'And it isn't only that. There's the partnership here, there's my cottage... Oh, the list is endless. I just can't see how it's all going to work out. In fact, if I'm honest, I'm not sure which way to turn.'

'First things first,' said Geraldine briskly. 'Face the facts. Fact number one is that you're pregnant. Fact number two is that the father doesn't yet know. I'd say the first thing you need to do is to tell him. Once you do so you may well find that all the other problems will resolve themselves. Tell me, this man—can you contact him easily?'

'Oh, yes,' Sara nodded weakly. 'Yes, I can.'

'In that case, why don't you make telling him the number one priority?'

Sara continued to stare at Geraldine, then she took a deep breath and stood. 'Yes, Geraldine,' she said at last, 'you're absolutely right. I'll tell him. I'll do it tonight. And thank you for listening.'

'That's all right,' said Geraldine. 'Hope I've been of

some help. It's the least I can do. After all, you've listened to enough of my troubles.'

It was almost dusk by the time Sara finally got away from Marshcombe House. Jean had just received the holiday photographs that she and Francis had taken in Canada and had been eager to show them to Sara. Under normal conditions Sara would have been delighted to sit and see the latest pictures of her cousin, David, his wife, Sue, and their children. As it was, with the possible exception of the shots of the new baby, which she almost devoured, she couldn't wait for the session to come to an end. She'd worked herself up to such a pitch that she just wanted to see Alex and get the whole thing over with.

The last thing she wanted, however, was for Jean and Francis to think that she wasn't interested in their photographs. Even after the pictures moved on from family shots to an extensive record of scenery and the places they'd visited she managed to maintain, she hoped, an enthusiastic interest.

'Well, that's the last one,' said Jean at last. 'It really was the most wonderful trip and it was lovely to be with the family again, even if it was only for a short time.'

'You did say they were planning to come here next year, didn't you?' said Sara.

'Yes.' Jean nodded then sighed. 'By then little Chloe will be over a year old.'

And I'll have a baby of around three months, thought Sara.

Jean stood up. 'Who'd like a cup of tea?' she said, and Sara couldn't help but notice that her eyes were suspiciously brighter than usual.

Shaking her head, Sara also rose to her feet. 'Not for me, thanks, Jean. I...I thought I'd go for a walk. I'll take Jason with me, if you like.' As she spoke she looked

towards the hearth where the elderly Labrador, hearing
his name, began to thump his tail noisily on the rug.

Moments later she was walking down the drive to the
road. Jason was padding by her side, his tongue lolling
in anticipation.

She cut across the fields to give Jason a good run,
before backtracking towards the mill stream. By the time
she reached the cottages her heart was thumping.

She tried desperately to imagine what Alex's reaction
to the news would be. Secretly, she already was cherish-
ing a hope that he'd be as pleased as she was. They'd
been getting on so well in the last few weeks and he'd
even begun to help her with plans for decorating and
furnishing the cottage. From time to time he still laughingly said that because the two cottages were so small
the only real solution was to knock them into one.

A soft mist had descended over the fields and mos-
quitoes hovered above the stream in a cloud, promising
heat the next day. By the time she rounded the corner of
the old mill the sun had slipped below the horizon and
the sky was a deep crimson wash. She expected to see
Alex's car parked outside his cottage, but to her dismay
there was no sign of it. Neither were the lamps lit inside
the house.

After fastening the lead onto Jason's collar, she approached the cottage and rang the bell. The notes echoed
emptily inside, confirming the fact that Alex was not at
home.

Her own cottage, in darkness, stood equally silent. She
felt a stab of disappointment. She'd prepared herself for
this moment—had been ready to tell him.

Sara crossed the road and sat for a while on the stone
wall bordering the stream. It was very quiet and there
were few people about. An elderly man passed her on
his way to the pub and nodded a greeting. A little later

a carload of teenagers roared over the bridge, shattering the peace of the summer twilight.

After half an hour she came to the conclusion that Alex was out for the evening, and with a sigh she began to make her way back into the village. As she approached Marshcombe House she found herself wondering if he might have gone there, but there was only her own car parked alongside her uncle's in the drive.

Still disappointed, she let herself into the house and took off Jason's lead. While the dog was lapping noisily at his bowl of water she called goodnight to Jean and Francis, who were watching television in the sitting-room, then made her way up to bed, reflecting as she did so that she would just have to wait until the next day before she told Alex the news.

The following day was Saturday and it was Sara's turn to take the emergency morning surgery. Only she, Poli and Sandie, the practice nurse, were on duty at the medical centre so there was still no opportunity to speak to Alex. She knew that Jean and Francis had invited him to lunch at Marshcombe House but she could hardly tell him the news as they all sat around the table. She allowed herself a wry little smile as she imagined the scene.

'Would you pass the salad, please, Francis? Oh, by the way, Alex, we're going to have a baby. No, I know we aren't married, but a lot of people aren't these days. Yes, I know I've just become a partner, but there's plenty of room for a carrycot in my consulting-room. I know because I've measured up. I did it after I'd measured for the curtains in the cottage I've just taken out a huge mortgage on.'

She felt hysterical laughter threatening to surface and had to force herself to concentrate on the patients' problems, which that morning ranged from a toddler with an ear infection, an asthmatic affected by the crops of rape seed in the fields around Longwood Chase and a young woman with a severe migraine.

She'd just seen her last patient out when Poli rang through to say there was one more, a temporary resident, who was filling in his form.

'Very well, Poli. Send him in when he's finished.'

She was flicking through the pages of the latest medical journal when there came a tap at her door. 'Come in,' she called.

A man came into the room, shutting the door behind him. He was of medium height and a slightly stocky build, with receding brown hair and a neatly trimmed beard. He looked strained and tired, as if he'd passed a sleepless night.

'Good morning, Doctor.'

'Good morning,' Sara nodded. 'Come in and sit down. I understand you're a temporary resident?'

'Yes. At the moment I am. I'm working here for the summer.'

'How may I help you?' As the man sat he passed his temporary resident form to Sara.

'I suffer from tennis elbow,' he said. 'The pain's killing me at the moment.'

'Have you had treatment for this before?'

'Yes, painkillers and once I had a cortisone injection.'

'Well, I'd better take a look at it for you, Mr...Mr...' Sara glanced at the top of the form. 'Mr. Lewis?'

'Yes, that's right.'

Sara stared at the form. 'Calvin Lewis?' she said.

The man nodded. 'Before you ask, yes, I am Geraldine Lewis's husband.'

'Oh, I see. Well, let's take a look at that arm, shall we?' Sara stood and as she moved round to examine the man's elbow she found herself trying to remember what

Geraldine had told her about her estranged husband. She didn't have to try too hard, however, for Calvin Lewis volunteered the information himself.

'We aren't living together at the moment,' he said as he rolled up the sleeve of the sweatshirt he was wearing. 'We've been living apart for about nine months now...but I've moved back into the area recently. I'm working at the local pub and living in—I was hoping that we could get back together again.' He winced as Sara found the painful part of his elbow.

'That's it, is it?' she asked. 'Sorry. Now, could you move your arm, please...this way and that way. Yes, that's it. Thank you. You can put your sleeve down again now. And do you think that's likely, Mr Lewis?' she asked, as she returned to her chair.

'Eh?' Calvin slowly and painfully eased his sleeve over his elbow.

'You said you were hoping you and your wife would get back together, and I asked if you thought that was likely.'

'Well, I did to start with,' he replied with a grunt. 'Now I'm not so sure.'

'Oh?' Sara looked up. 'And why is that?'

'Well, she's got herself this fancy man. Doesn't look like she wants to know me now. I suppose it serves me right, but there you are...' He gave a helpless shrug then winced again as fresh pain hit him.

'I'm going to give you some painkillers to take over the weekend, Mr Lewis,' said Sara, 'but I want to see you again on Tuesday. If your elbow isn't any better by then I shall want to give you another cortisone injection.'

'Yes, all right, Doctor. Thank you.' He was silent while Sara entered details into her computer, but while she was waiting for the prescription to print he said, 'It will be you I'll see on Tuesday, won't it?'

'Hopefully, yes,' Sara said, 'but if for any reason I'm not available one of my partners will see you.' When he remained silent she tore off the prescription and handed it to him. 'Do you have a problem with that, Mr Lewis?' she asked.

'Well,' he said, 'to be honest, I would rather it was you, Doctor, or maybe Dr Rossington. I was glad it was you today. I didn't want to see Dr Mason.'

'Oh?' Sara looked up in surprise. It was so unusual to hear anyone say anything against Alex. 'Why's that?' she asked curiously before she could stop herself.

'Well, it wouldn't seem right somehow under the circumstances, would it? And, you never know, I might not be able to restrain myself. Tennis elbow or no tennis elbow, I might just end up punching him on the nose.'

'I'm sorry, Mr Lewis.' Sara gave a puzzled laugh. 'I'm afraid you'll have to enlighten me. I haven't a clue what you mean.'

'Well, it's him, isn't it?' He stared at Sara as if she was a little slow on the uptake.

'What is?' She frowned.

'Him. The chap I was telling you about. I thought you'd have known, you working with them both and all that. It's him,' he repeated patiently as, with an awful possibility stirring in her mind, Sara continued to stare at him. 'Your Dr Mason. That's her fancy man, the one she's seeing at the moment—the reason she's not interested in taking me back.'

'Mr Lewis.' Sara swallowed. 'I think you'll find you're making a mistake. I'm sure your wife...Geraldine isn't involved with Alex...Dr Mason.'

'Well, I tell you they are. She was with him last night. Ask them yourself. I went round to her place to try and reason with her and he arrived in that fancy red Golf of his while I was there. She'd just told me that she was seeing him and that she wanted to try and make a go of things with him, then he arrived and she asked me to leave. It was a shock, I can tell you. I had a dreadful night, what with the pain from this elbow and imagining the two of them together. It was horrendous.'

Sara didn't know how she kept her composure until Calvin Lewis had left her consulting-room, but somehow she did. After he'd gone she sat for a long time, simply staring at the door.

Her brain was in chaos. Alex and Geraldine? Surely not. But was it so improbable? Had she not also thought the same thing once? But then, having convinced herself she'd been mistaken, she'd put the whole possibility out of her mind. Had she been wrong to do so? Had her first inclinations, in fact, been correct?

Of course not, she told herself briskly. The whole thing was preposterous.

What was it Calvin Lewis had said? That he'd been at Geraldine's house when Alex had arrived? He'd even gone on to give an accurate description of his car.

It was true that Alex had been out the previous evening when she herself had tried to find him but, surely, if he'd gone to see Geraldine there must have been some other explanation. Perhaps he'd gone to see her about practice business. Yes, that must have been it. That was far more likely.

If that was the case, why hadn't he dealt with it during working hours? It wasn't like Alex to take business matters to someone's home. And hadn't Calvin said that Geraldine had actually told him that Alex was the new man in her life?

What had Geraldine told her? Frantically Sara began to search her memory. She'd told her all about Calvin and why they had parted. She'd said there was a new man in her life. She'd told Sara that almost at the beginning when she'd first come to the practice. Sara could recall it now.

Geraldine had said that it was very early days in the relationship and she didn't want to rush things. She, Sara, intuitively thinking at the time that Alex might be the man, had asked her how early, and Geraldine's reply had been that she'd only seen him—what? Twice? Yes, twice, that was what she'd said. Sara remembered joking about it and saying, 'Oh, that early!' or words to that effect. She'd felt relief at that moment because she felt that had ruled out Alex because Geraldine and Alex saw each other all the time.

Maybe she'd been wrong. Maybe what Geraldine had meant was that she'd only had two actual dates with her new man.

Was it Alex? Could it be possible? Geraldine was certainly a very attractive woman and she was separated from her husband, which left her more or less free to date whom she pleased.

Alex was also free, and charming, and attractive, as Sara herself knew only too well. When he'd first come to Longwood Chase it would have been around the time that Geraldine had been left by Calvin. And shortly after the time that she and Alex had parted. Had they been two lonely people—two vulnerable people—seeking comfort from each other?

Sara could see, only too easily, how it could have happened. But what about afterwards—what about when she had come back onto the scene? Alex had given the impression right from the start that he'd have liked nothing better than for them to get back together again.

At least, that had been her interpretation. Could it be that she'd misread that situation as well?

She was shifting uneasily in her chair when the intercom sounded.

'Yes, Poli?' she said.

'That's the last, Dr Denton.'

'Very well, Poli. Thank you. You get off home now. Have a nice weekend. I'll take the pager with me. I'm on call this afternoon.'

She flicked the intercom switch and moments later she heard Poli and Sandie leave the building. She, however, didn't move but continued to sit behind her desk, wrestling with her thoughts—thoughts which were becoming increasingly disturbing by the minute.

Maybe she *had* misread the situation. Maybe Alex hadn't wanted to resume their relationship. After all, at first wasn't that what she, too, had wanted? She'd even told him that if she were to become a partner their relationship had to remain strictly professional. And she'd meant it.

Could she blame him if he'd looked elsewhere? If that was the case, why was she upset?

She stood abruptly, walked to the window and with unseeing eyes stood, looking out.

She was upset because somewhere along the line it had all changed. He'd even slept with her, for goodness' sake. Would he have done that if he was involved with someone else?

On the other hand, had that night they'd spent together simply been a direct result of the circumstances at the time and the trauma surrounding the missing child, and had she not been as much to blame for it as he had?

At some point she had wanted Alex back. She wasn't sure exactly when that moment had been, but it had happened. But what of Alex—what did he want? She'd been almost sure he was feeling the same way as her.

Whose idea had it been that they started their relationship all over again? That had been her, she thought uneasily, but only after Alex had indicated that he would have been happy for them to move in together again. Maybe he'd been annoyed that she had suggested caution, so annoyed that he'd renewed a liaison with Geraldine.

But he hadn't seemed to be annoyed. He'd even given the impression of being delighted that she'd bought the cottage next door to his and had persisted with ongoing suggestions of knocking the two cottages into one. On the other hand, perhaps that had all been simply a joke.

Now the whole picture had changed yet again because she was pregnant. She'd just begun to convince herself that Alex might be pleased by this development, but that had been before she'd known of his involvement with Geraldine.

Suppose, just like that other time, he was horrified? Suppose he quite simply didn't ever want the commitment of marriage or a baby?

Or, and somehow this prospect was even worse, suppose he was smitten by his conscience? The last thing she wanted was for Alex to come back to her just because of the coming baby.

No, she thought as she at last turned away from the window, the only possible reason for a reconciliation would be because he loved her and her only, because she loved him and because they both wanted to make a home for the coming baby. And if none of those conditions applied then she would quite simply live alone and bring the child up on her own.

CHAPTER ELEVEN

SARA was quite late by the time she finally reached Marshcombe House, and Alex's car was already parked on the drive.

On entering the house, she found that the others had waited lunch for her.

'Sorry I'm late,' she said, carefully avoiding Alex's eye as she joined them in the conservatory, where they were enjoying a pre-lunch drink.

'Heavy morning?' asked Francis sympathetically.

'Not particularly,' said Sara. 'I had a last-minute patient—a temporary resident.' She paused and on a sudden impulse said, 'Actually, it was Geraldine Lewis's husband, Calvin.'

'Are they back together again?' asked Jean in surprise.

Sara shook her head. 'Not as far as I know. I understand he's working at the Red Lion and living there as well.'

'What happened to the woman he went off with?' asked Francis.

'She's tired of him, apparently, and threw him out,' said Sara with a little shrug.

'Well!' said Jean. 'After all that. At one time he was desperate for a divorce. Do you think he wants to go back to Geraldine now?'

'Question is—would she want him back?' said Francis with a short laugh. Getting to his feet, he said, 'Sara, my dear, what can I get you to drink? A sherry?'

She hesitated. 'Er...no, I think just a mineral water, please. I'm on call,' she added. As Francis disappeared inside the house to fetch her drink she at last allowed herself a quick glance in Alex's direction to see what his reaction had been to the conversation. His expression was inscrutable, however, as he sipped his drink, giving away nothing of his own feelings.

Suddenly she felt a surge of anger wash over her. How dared he sit there so unconcerned when all the time he'd not only been chatting her up but stringing Geraldine along into the bargain.

Or had it been the other way round? Had he been chatting up Geraldine and stringing her, Sara, along? She grew so incensed the more she thought about it that when Alex asked her some ordinary, mundane question about the practice she almost bit his head off.

He looked shocked at her uncharacteristic reaction but by then they were all moving in to the dining-room for lunch so he didn't pursue the matter.

There was a rather strained atmosphere after that as Sara pointedly ignored Alex. As Jean and Francis became aware of the situation Francis vainly attempted a jovial approach to lighten the hidden tensions. They'd almost finished the meal when they were suddenly interrupted by the frantic ringing of the doorbell. Jean hurried into the hall to answer it.

'No doubt someone has decided to have a baby or a heart attack,' said Francis wearily. 'Folk have no sense of timing over these things. The fact it's the weekend means absolutely nothing.'

A moment later Jean came back into the room. 'It's a boy,' she said. 'He says his name is Grant Turvey.'

As Francis gave a low groan Sara said, 'Does he want a doctor, Jean?'

'He says it's for his brother. Apparently, the pair of them were playing up in the derelict farm buildings at

the Morris place, and from what I can make out, the boy
has had an accident.'

Sara threw down her napkin and hurried out into the
hall, to find Grant Turvey in jeans and T-shirt, looking
frightened and uncomfortable.

'What is it, Grant?' asked Sara. 'What's happened?'

'It was me and Liam, miss. We was playing comman-
dos up at Morris's farm. Liam climbed onto the roof
and...and...'

Aware that Alex had followed her into the hall, Sara
crouched in front of the white-faced boy. 'What happened, Grant? Did Liam fall?'

'Yes.' Grant's voice was barely more than a whisper
but he nodded vigorously.

'Is he on the ground?' asked Alex, over Sara's shoulder.

'I don't know... The roof fell in... He went through,'
said Grant distractedly. 'I couldn't get to him—it's all
barred up.'

'All right,' said Sara. 'I'll come up there now.'

'I'll come with you,' said Alex.

'I'm sure I can manage,' she replied coolly, as she
picked up her medical bag from the hall table where
she'd left it.

'You may need some help, getting in,' Alex replied.

She couldn't really argue with that, but as they hurried
from Marshcombe House she said, 'Should we call the
emergency services?'

'Not yet,' Alex replied. 'We need to see what the situation is first. Liam may be perfectly all right. We'd look
pretty silly, calling the police, the fire service and an
ambulance—only to find he's sitting inside the house,
simply waiting to be let out, wouldn't we, Grant?'

'I think he might be hurt,' said Grant. 'He didn't answer me when I called—but we don't need the police, do we?' he said anxiously.

'We'll see,' said Alex. 'Come on, we'll take my car.'

Sara didn't argue with him over that, content to let him drive out of the village and up the rough, derelict track to the old Morris place. She was only too aware of the fact that her heart was still heavy with anguish over what she'd learnt that morning, and that every time she looked at Alex it was as if a knife twisted inside her as she thought of how he'd two-timed her.

She could still hardly believe it of him, but she now not only had Geraldine's word for it that there was a new man in her life but also that of Calvin who'd gone one stage further, by naming the man.

They were mostly silent on the drive and Grant remained white-faced and anxious. It had rained again in the night, not light summer showers this time but heavy, almost torrential rain that had fallen in sheets, leaving huge puddles in the rough tracks and slowing their progress considerably. The rain hadn't even cleared the air and the day was sullen and overcast, with great banks of dark cloud gathering in the west as if preparing for a fresh onslaught.

As the car bumped its way over the deep grooves, slicing through the puddles and sending up great sprays of water, they passed Matt Jenkins's cottage. The old man was peering out of his front window at them. Sara waved to him but he didn't wave back.

'He must wonder what on earth is going on,' said Alex grimly.

'Grant,' said Sara suddenly, turning her head to speak to the boy in the back seat of the car, 'does your mum know where you and Liam had gone to play?'

Grant shook his head. 'No,' he admitted sheepishly. 'We aren't allowed up there.'

'Should we call her on the mobile?' Sara threw a glance at Alex.

He shook his head. 'No, let's see what the situation is first. No point worrying her unnecessarily. There's been enough anxiety around here lately to last for a very long time.'

The disused farm buildings consisted of the farmhouse itself, a huge barn and a collection of outbuildings, stables and pigsties. The whole place had an empty, forlorn look about it. The house windows were boarded up and part of the roof of the barn was missing, its rafters black and charred from a recent fire started by vandals. A piece of tarpaulin, covering the doorway to the stable, flapped in the breeze and somewhere from within the buildings a creaking noise could be heard. Apart from that there was silence.

As they climbed from the car Alex looked at Grant. 'Which way?' he said.

'Over there.' The boy pointed to the outhouses behind the farmhouse. Together they crossed the farmyard, Sara thinking as they went how eerie the place seemed. The doors and windows of the building were barred with thick wooden battening, obviously to deter vandals. Alex tried to peer between the battens through the dirty glass into the room beyond.

'Can you see anything?' asked Sara.

'Not a thing. Where were you playing?' Alex turned and looked at Grant.

'Up there.' He pointed to the flat roof of the two-storey outhouse. 'There's a hayloft up there.'

'How did you get up there?' Alex stood back, craning his neck.

'Over there... We climbed along the roof of the pigsty then up the pipe to the roof of the outhouse. That's when it gave way and Liam fell through.'

'Right.' Alex took a deep breath. 'Looks like I'd better do the same.'

'Alex, for God's sake, be careful,' said Sara urgently.

'I'm only going to have a look,' he said. 'You stay here—and you,' he added to Grant.

Sara and Grant watched as Alex climbed onto the roof of the pigsty. He balanced himself carefully as he walked along the top, then climbed up a piece of drainpipe to the flat roof of the outhouse. Dropping on all fours, he began to inch forward cautiously.

'Alex, please, be careful,' called Sara. 'If you fall through as well...'

'I'm all right,' Alex called back.

'Can you see him?' called Grant. 'Can you see Liam?'

There was no reply from Alex, and he'd now moved out of their line of vision. In an agony of suspense they waited until finally Sara could bear it no longer.

'Alex,' she shouted. 'Where are you?'

When there was still no reply she called, 'I'm coming up.'

'No, don't do that. I'm coming down.' Alex's head suddenly appeared again above the edge of the roof.

'Did you see him?' asked Grant, his eyes dark with fear in his white face as Alex dropped to the roof of the pigsty and began to walk back towards them.

'Yes.' Alex nodded as he slid to the ground. 'Yes, he's in there.'

'Is he all right?' gasped Grant.

'Hard to tell,' said Alex. 'Probably unconscious. Sara, would you phone the emergency services, please? We can't get him out on our own. I think I can probably get down to him, but I need my bag.' He turned and began to cross the yard to his car.

Sara took her mobile phone from her pocket and began to dial the emergency numbers—the police first to explain the situation, give the location and ask for assistance, then the ambulance.

'Do you think he's dead?' Grant was beside her, frantically tugging at her sleeve. 'He is, isn't he? He's dead.'

'We don't know that, Grant,' said Sara. 'We must just wait while Dr Mason goes down to him.'

And that was all they could do. They watched helplessly while Alex scaled the buildings again, this time lowering himself through the dangerous remains of the roof to the trapped boy.

'We're always fighting,' muttered Grant, suddenly gnawing at his thumbnail as they waited, 'but I don't want him to die.'

'He might be all right, Grant,' said Sara, trying to comfort and reassure the boy. 'Dr Mason will do all he can.'

The waiting seemed interminable and there was no further sound from Alex. At last Grant lifted his head. 'Listen,' he said.

Sara heard it then, the unmistakable wail of a police siren. Minutes later a police car and a rescue Land Rover roared into the farmyard, shattering the silence and causing a couple of pigeons to rise flapping and squawking from the rafters of the old barn.

'What's the gen, miss?' One of the policeman climbed out of the car and walked towards them, adjusting his cap.

'I'm Dr Denton,' Sara replied. 'My colleague, Dr Mason, is inside that building over there. He had to lower himself through the roof to get to an injured boy. There was no other way in because all the doors and windows are boarded up.'

'How did the boy get in there?' asked the policeman suspiciously, eyeing Grant up and down.

'He was playing on the roof when it fell in,' said Sara.

'Looks like our first job, then,' said the policeman, 'is to remove those barricades.'

The boarding was removed in a remarkably short space of time. After telling Grant to stay with one of the police crew, Sara followed two other policemen into the outhouse.

It was dark and musty inside, with a curiously pungent smell about it that suggested it had at one time been used to store pesticides. The floor was dirty and choked with rubbish, straw and pieces of polythene. In the far corner of one of the rooms narrow wooden stairs, festooned with cobwebs, led to the upper floor.

As they approached, Alex's face appeared above them and Sara felt an overwhelming pang of relief.

'He's up here,' said Alex.

'Is he alive?' asked Sara, as she climbed the stairs, with the policemen behind her.

'Yes.' Alex nodded and led the way into a second room, which was curiously light because daylight poured through a large opening in the roof. 'He was knocked unconscious in the fall, but he's come round now. He's badly injured,' he said quietly.

Liam was lying where he'd fallen in the midst of the debris from the roof. His face was very white and there was dirt on one cheek and blood on the other. Alex had covered him with his jacket. 'I've given him a painkilling shot,' he said, as Sara sank to her knees beside the boy.

'What are his injuries?' asked one of the policemen.

'One of his legs is broken,' said Alex. 'Cuts and grazes, of course, and I suspect internal injuries, but it's his back I'm worried about. He doesn't seem to have any feeling in his legs. I want him immobilised as much as possible before he's moved.'

'The ambulance is on its way,' replied the policeman. 'The paramedics will have the equipment you need.'

'Hello, miss. What you doing here?'

Sara looked down and saw that Liam had opened his eyes and was staring at her in surprise.

'Hello, Liam,' she said. 'You've taken a nasty tumble through the roof.'

'How did you know?' he said.

'Grant came and told us,' Sara replied, gently stroking the boy's forehead.

'Is my mum here as well?' asked Liam.

'No,' Sara replied, 'but there'll be an ambulance coming in a moment to take you to hospital. I'll come with you, Dr Mason will bring Grant and we'll phone your mum and let her know what's happening so that she can go straight to the hospital.'

That seemed to satisfy the boy and he closed his eyes again.

A short time later the sound of a klaxon heralded the arrival of the ambulance. While Alex went down to talk to the paramedics and tell them what equipment was needed Sara continued to sit beside the injured boy, periodically checking his pulse.

When Alex returned with the two paramedics they inserted a cannula into a vein in the boy's hand then set up a saline drip to replace any fluids which might have been lost through internal bleeding.

Next they immobilised the boy's neck in a collar and secured his fractured leg between two splints, before fastening him on a stretcher so that there would be the least amount of movement while he was being transported to the hospital. Then Alex, the paramedics and a policeman carried Liam gently down the stairs, and Sara went to find Grant.

She found the boy in a police car in the company of

a WPC. He looked fearful and his eyes and nose were red, as if he'd been crying.

'Is he OK?' he asked, looking over Sara's shoulder to the outhouses where the men had just come into view with Liam on the stretcher.

'Hopefully, yes, Grant,' Sara replied. 'They'll take him to hospital now, but I want to ring your mum to tell her what has happened. Can you tell me your phone number?'

At mention of his mother Grant's face had blanched even more, but he managed to mumble his phone number to Sara who dialled it on her mobile phone. She'd just begun to think that Linda Turvey wasn't at home when, on the twentieth ring, she answered.

'Yes?' she yelled.

Sara winced. 'Mrs Turvey?' she asked.

'Yes. Who's that?'

'It's Dr Denton, Mrs Turvey.'

'Oh?' Her tone changed slightly.

'I don't want to alarm you too much, Mrs Turvey,' Sara went on, 'but I'm afraid that Liam has had an accident—'

That was as far as she got. Linda cut her short. 'What do you mean—an accident? Where is he? What's happened to him? Is Grant with him?'

Sara took a deep breath. 'Liam has been injured, Mrs Turvey. We don't know yet quite how badly, but he's being taken to St Benedict's Hospital. And, yes, Grant is here too.'

'Where are you? Where did this accident happen?'

'We are up at the old Morris farm.'

'What!'

Sara jumped and rapidly moved the phone away from her ear as Linda's screech was heard, not only by herself but by Grant and the WPC.

'I've told those boys time and time again they aren't to go up there. It's dangerous. What happened to him?' Linda Turvey demanded.

'He had a fall... He was climbing...'

'I'll give him climbing—he'll wish he'd never been born when I get hold of him. Where's Grant? Let me speak to Grant.'

Sara glanced at the boy and saw the dread in his eyes. 'I have to go, Mrs Turvey,' said Sara. 'Can I suggest you make your way to the hospital and we'll meet you there?'

Grant visibly sagged with relief as Sara replaced the aerial on her mobile phone. 'I'm going in the ambulance with Liam,' she said, 'but Dr Mason will bring you to the hospital in his car.'

Leaving Grant with the WPC, Sara hurried across to the rear of the ambulance.

'He's pretty stable,' said Alex. 'See you at St Benedict's.'

Sara scrambled aboard with one of the paramedics, while the other fastened the doors and Alex stood watching. For the briefest of moments before the ambulance carried her out of his line of vision, Sara's gaze met his, and in that instant she saw unmistakable puzzlement in his eyes and she knew he was still trying to fathom the reason for her coolness towards him.

The next hour was frantic, with their arrival at the hospital, Liam being whisked away into Casualty and the arrival of Alex and Grant—followed very soon afterwards by that of Linda Turvey and her boyfriend.

Surprisingly, Linda was quiet. Instead of clouting Grant, which Sara had feared she might do, she hugged him fiercely. It seemed that during her ride to the hospital the seriousness of the situation had had time to sink in.

'I'm sorry, Mum.' Grant buried his face against his mother's T-shirt.

'How is he?' Linda's eyes met Sara's over Grant's head, and Sara recognised once again that unspeakable dread which she'd last seen in Marilyn Jones's eyes. 'Is he...?'

'No, Linda,' she said gently. 'It's all right, he's alive. Just tell the nurse you've arrived. I'm sure they'll let you see him soon.' As Linda disappeared into Reception her boyfriend looked at Grant.

'Come on, mate,' he said gruffly. 'Let's go and get ourselves a Coke and a Mars bar while we're waiting, shall we?' He glanced up at Sara—and at Alex, who'd just joined them in the hospital foyer. 'Thanks a lot,' he said. Lowering his voice, he said, 'Is he going to be all right?'

'We hope so,' Alex replied. 'He has some serious injuries but, well, he's in good hands now. They'll do their best to sort him out.' He glanced at Sara. 'Shall we go now?'

She nodded. 'Bye, Grant,' she said, then together she and Alex made their way to the hospital car park.

They didn't go straight back to Marshcombe House. Instead, Alex drove to the Mill Cottages and stopped in front of number one. When Sara turned and looked questioningly at him he switched off the engine. Leaning back in his seat, he said, 'Right, Sara, what's this all about?'

'What?' she said coolly.

'Well, I gather from your manner towards me this morning that I've done something to upset you.' When Sara remained silent he went on, 'I've wracked my brains but I'm damned if I can think what it is.'

Slowly she turned and looked at him. 'Are you trying to tell me that you really don't know?' she said.

'Well, if I did I don't think we'd be sitting here like

this. Please, Sara, whatever it is you'll have to tell me because I can't put it right unless I do know.'

She was silent for a long moment then, staring straight ahead through the windscreen, she said, 'You gave me to understand that where our relationship was concerned we were going to go right back to square one and start again.'

'Yes.' Alex frowned. 'That's right. That's exactly what we agreed. No pressures, no hassle and we'd take things very slowly—that's what we said. I'm sorry, Sara, I still don't see what the problem is.'

'Well, maybe I'm a bit thick or something,' she went on bitterly, 'because, even though we didn't actually spell it out, I imagined that arrangement would naturally exclude any other relationships. Maybe that was naïve of me. I'm sorry...' she shrugged '...but that's how I thought it would be.'

'But that's right. That's how I saw things as well.' Alex looked bewildered. 'After all, let's face it, there's no way we're going to rebuild our relationship otherwise.'

Turning her head, she stared at him. As if things weren't bad enough, it looked as if he intended to lie to her as well.

'Sara,' he said, 'what is it? What's wrong? Why are you looking at me like that?' Leaning forward, he tried to take her hand but she snatched it away angrily.

'Please, Alex,' she said, turning and fumbling for the doorcatch, 'don't insult my intelligence, by lying to me. There really isn't any point because I know the truth.'

'What truth, for goodness' sake?' He scrambled out of the car and they faced each other across the bonnet.

'Oh, don't pretend you don't know what I mean,' she cried. 'I was here last night, looking for you. Where were you?'

He still looked bewildered. 'No,' she went on, 'you needn't bother to think up more lies because I know where you were. I know exactly where you were. You were with Geraldine Lewis. And I know that for a fact, Alex, so you needn't bother to try and deny it!'

CHAPTER TWELVE

SARA turned away sharply, quite prepared now to walk back to Marshcombe House, but within seconds Alex was in front of her, barring her way.

'Alex...please...' She tried to pass him but he stopped her.

'No,' he said. 'I let you get away from me once before. It was the biggest mistake of my life and one I don't intend to repeat.'

'But—'

'Please, Sara...please.'

Helplessly she stared at him.

'Come into the cottage.' He paused as an elderly lady walked past them, her expression one of curiosity. 'I really can't imagine what the locals would make of two of their doctors brawling in public,' he said as the woman walked on up the road.

With a sigh Sara turned reluctantly and followed him into number one, Mill Cottages.

'I need to talk to you,' he said as he shut the front door behind them. 'I need to explain. Come through to the kitchen.'

Numbly she allowed herself to be swept along, but at the same time she doubted that anything he said by way of explanation could change things. He'd been the new man in Geraldine's life, and he'd lied to her. Nothing could change that.

Wearily she sat at the kitchen table while Alex leaned against the dresser.

'First of all,' he said, 'can I remind you that I still love you? To be honest, Sara, I don't think I ever stopped loving you—'

'How can you say that,' she demanded, staring at him in growing exasperation, 'when all the time you and Geraldine—?'

'Sara, I did go and see Geraldine last night, but not for the reason you think. To be honest, I didn't realise you knew about Geraldine.'

'Hah! So, what are you saying?' She continued to stare at him, astonished at his apparent arrogance. 'That if I'd known it would have made everything all right? Or was it simply a case of as long as I didn't find out you could go on, getting away with it?'

'No. You don't understand. It wasn't like that with Geraldine.'

'Well, it might not have been for you,' Sara retorted, 'but it certainly was for her.'

'But I didn't know that,' he said quietly. 'Honestly, Sara, you must believe me. I didn't know.'

'Well, I find that very hard to believe.' With an angry little gesture Sara turned away, then she added quickly, 'Geraldine was full of it.'

'You mean *she* told you?' Alex looked startled. 'What did she say, for heaven's sake?'

'She told me there was a gorgeous new man in her life. That was right at the beginning—soon after I came to the village. She also told me,' Sara went on, while Alex remained in a sort of stunned silence, 'that she was being very cautious about the whole thing, especially in view of what had happened with her husband. What she didn't tell me, however, was who this gorgeous new man was—I only wish to hell that she had!' she added bitterly. 'I tell you now, Alex, if she had, things between you and I would have been very different.'

Alex was frowning now. Ignoring her comment, he said, 'Did you tell Geraldine about us?'

'Not exactly,' she replied shortly. With a little shrug she went on, 'I told her there had been someone in my life, that we'd lived together for two years but that we'd parted and I'd gone abroad. I also told her that I'd met up with this man again since coming back to this country.'

'But you didn't say it was me?'

'No. Because you told me not to. You told me not to tell any of the staff. I wondered why you said that at the time. Now I know!'

'No, Sara. You don't.' Alex half turned away in exasperation. 'I told you not to let on to the staff because I feared gossip and the effect that might have on you. I thought it might affect your decision to join the partnership. I feared it might put you off. And that was the only reason. I swear it.'

He paused. When Sara didn't answer he said, 'As far as Geraldine is concerned, please, will you let me explain.'

He took her silence for assent and carried on swiftly before she tried to stop him. 'When I first came to Longwood Chase Geraldine was in a very low, vulnerable state, after being left by her husband, Calvin. She chose to confide in me and I felt sorry for her. I asked her out for a meal one night.'

When Sara looked up sharply he went on, 'You have to remember, Sara, that at that time, as far as I knew, our relationship was at an end. You'd made that quite plain when you left and went to Saudi Arabia.'

'I know that,' said Sara quickly, 'just as I accept that at the time you were perfectly at liberty to go out with whomever you chose. It was later that I'm bothered about. After I returned.'

'I'm coming to that,' said Alex patiently. 'As I was saying, I took Geraldine out for a meal, more to cheer her up than anything else.'

'Were you attracted to her at that time?'

'Geraldine is a very attractive woman,' Alex replied, 'but, to answer your question, no, I wasn't attracted to her—at least, not in the way you mean.'

'Don't try—'

'No, Sara, listen. Let me finish. Geraldine isn't my type—it's as simple as that.'

'So you led her on?' demanded Sara. 'Is that what you're saying?'

'No. I didn't lead her on.'

'You must have done for her to believe there was a possibility you and she could make a go of a relationship.'

'I didn't know for sure she felt that way—not until last night,' said Alex quietly.

'So you admit you were with her last night?'

'I told you I went to see her last night. She phoned and asked me over for supper. I tried to refuse and she became agitated. It was then, on the phone, that my suspicions were confirmed as to how she was really feeling.'

'So you'd suspected before?'

'Yes. Like I say, I took her out to dinner just once, then I went to her place for a meal—again just once. It was then that I began to have an inkling that she might be getting fond of me. Soon after that you arrived. I didn't see Geraldine again after that. Apart from at work, of course.

'After you and I decided we were going to try and make a go of things again,' he carried on after a moment, 'I attempted to tell Geraldine one day at work that we wouldn't be going out together again. She wouldn't listen. She became very upset and walked out of my room.'

Sara remained silent as she remembered the day she'd seen Geraldine and wondered what Alex had said to her to upset her.

'Everything seemed to go quiet after that,' Alex continued after a moment, 'and I thought she'd got over it, especially when her husband turned up again. I think she's still in love with Calvin and he with her—but when she asked me over to her house again last night I knew I had to do something about it.'

He paused and ran his fingers through his hair in a faintly distracted way, before continuing. 'When I arrived Calvin Lewis was there. It was pretty embarrassing, I can tell you. Geraldine practically threw him out, and then I had to tell her that there was never going to be any sort of relationship between us because I was in love with you and always had been.'

Sara stared at him. 'You told her that?' she said at last, and her voice was little more than a whisper.

'Yes,' he said. 'She knows now. Like you say, she already knew there was someone in your life—she actually confirmed that last night—but she didn't know that someone was me.'

For a moment Sara simply didn't know what to say, then another possibility occurred to her. She'd confessed to Geraldine that she was pregnant. Last night Geraldine must have put two and two together and realised that Alex was the father of her coming child.

Had she told him?

Apparently not, otherwise by now Alex would have revealed that he knew. Suddenly, as everything began to fall into place, Sara started to feel ashamed that she had doubted him so much.

'Alex...' she began. 'I don't know what to say...I really don't...'

'Then don't say anything.' He pushed himself away

from the dresser to stand in front of her, take her hands and draw her to her feet.

'But I doubted you. I shouldn't have done that. I'm sorry.'

He chuckled. 'Under the circumstances, I can hardly blame you. It must have looked pretty suspicious to you.'

'Yes, well...but I should have trusted you.' She paused. 'How was Geraldine when you left her?'

'She was OK. She understood, I think, that anything she thought there had been, had been in her own head. I think, however, that, by asking her out when I did, I helped to restore her confidence at a time when it was at a very low ebb, and if that was the case I'm glad.'

'Do you think she and Calvin will get back together again?'

'Who knows?' Alex shrugged. 'I'd like to think they've got a chance, but at this precise moment I'm far more concerned about our relationship than Geraldine's and Calvin's.'

As he spoke he searched her face hungrily, as if desperate for some sign from her.

'You see, I'm getting rather impatient,' he went on. 'Oh, I know we said we'd take things slowly and for a time there I was happy to go along with that, but I'm getting fed up with that now.

'I don't want any more secrecy, Sara. I want to tell everyone that you're my girl. I love you and I want everyone to know it. I want to shout it from the rooftops. I want to knock that wall down over there so that our two cottages are one. I want us to be one. I want you to be my wife, Sara. I love you. I guess I always have, and I know I always will. I let you go once and it was the biggest mistake of my life.' As he'd been speaking he'd taken her face between his hands. His eyes gazed deeply into hers and his thumbs caressed her cheeks as his fingers became entangled in her hair.

'You said you weren't ready for commitment...'

'That was then. In the last year I've had a lot of time to think, and I've come to the conclusion you can't have all the pleasure without some sort of commitment.'

'We had differences, Alex, about what we wanted...'

'Crazy, stupid things that, with a bit of thought, could have easily been settled and worked through...'

'Things like our careers, and if we had children who'd look after them...'

'Things that would be worked out as and when they happened. If we had a child we'd work out between us what would be best—for us and for our child.

'Sara.' He tilted her face. 'Please put me out of my misery. Please tell me that you love me.'

'Oh, Alex, I do. I do love you. I've been so miserable without you.'

'And you will marry me?'

'Yes, of course I'll marry you.'

'And there's no need for any more of this waiting, for this taking things slowly...?'

'Actually, Alex...' Sara took a deep breath. 'I don't think this is an appropriate time for us to be taking things slowly. If we're going to get married now is probably a very good time to do so... In fact, I'd say, probably sooner rather than later.'

He stared at her, not quite understanding at first. Then he read the meaning behind her expression. 'You mean...?' he whispered, as the truth slowly dawned on him.

'Yes,' she said apprehensively, not entirely sure how he'd react and still mindful of the past. 'I guess we have to put it down to midnight impatience but, yes, it's true. We're going to have a baby.'

His shout of delight was probably heard by the entire neighbourhood as he caught her up and whirled her around. Then he set her down again and enfolded her in his arms, sealing their future with a deep, lingering kiss.

'You are pleased?' she asked anxiously, when at last he released her. 'About the baby?'

'Of course,' he said firmly. He added gently, 'Didn't you think I would be?'

'I really didn't know what to think,' she admitted. 'All I could think of was that last time—you know—when I thought I might be pregnant. I know in the end it turned out to be a false alarm but, well, you weren't exactly over the moon, Alex.'

'The circumstances were very different then.' There was a note of protest in his voice. 'We were only living together before and you'd only just qualified...'

'I thought you didn't want children at all.'

'Of course I want children,' he said, drawing her into his arms again. 'I realise that now. Even more important, I now know I want to be married. If there was one thing our separation taught me it was that I should never have let you go.'

'Do you really mean that, Alex?' she whispered.

'Of course I do. I love you, Sara. I want you to be my wife. You do love me, don't you?'

'Yes, Alex. Oh, yes,' she said with a sigh, as she lifted her face for his kiss. 'With all my heart.'

Two hours later they sat outside Marshcombe House in Alex's car, summoning the courage to go inside and tell Jean and Francis their news.

'I think they'll be over the moon,' said Alex at last. 'Especially Jean. You know how she is about babies.'

'Yes, I know,' said Sara, but there was an element of doubt in her voice. 'To be honest with you, it's Francis that worries me most. I can't imagine what he's going to say. Let's face it, Alex, the ink on the partnership contract is barely dry.'

'Surely it won't make a lot of difference?' Alex turned in his seat to face her. The excitement and joy was still evident in his eyes in the aftermath of the last two hours, which they'd spent in bed. 'You'll probably be able to work for a time, then take maternity leave. After that...' He shrugged. 'Well, you told me that modern mums go straight back to work these days...'

'I know, Alex,' she said quietly. 'I know that's what I said, just as I know you always said that no child of ours would be looked after by strangers.'

'I guess I was being pretty unrealistic,' muttered Alex.

'I don't know so much,' said Sara slowly. When Alex threw her a surprised look she went on, 'Just lately events that have happened have really made me think, and I've come to realise that those first few years of a child's life are very precious. They must go so fast and they can never be repeated. On the other hand, careers can't just be abandoned, practically or financially...'

'So, what are you saying?'

'I think some sort of middle course is the answer. Maybe part-time work, if it's possible, until the child is at least old enough for nursery school.'

Alex chuckled. 'Well, maybe we'd better go and see if Francis agrees with you.'

'Have you told him?'

It was the following Monday morning and Geraldine had come into Sara's consulting-room, shut the door behind her and was facing Sara across the desk.

Sara swallowed. 'Yes,' she said. 'I have told him.'

'What did he say?' The guarded, slightly hostile look which had been in Geraldine's eyes when she'd first en-

tered the room had been replaced by an expression that
was almost wistful.

'He was delighted,' said Sara simply.

Geraldine nodded. 'I thought he would be,' she said.
'So, are you getting married?'

'Yes, very soon.' Sara hesitated, then said, 'Thank you,
Geraldine, for not telling Alex. About the baby, I
mean...'

'I told you,' Geraldine said, 'confidentiality is my middle name.' There was a touch of regret, almost bitterness,
in her voice.

'Geraldine.' Sara took a deep breath. It had to be said.
'I honestly didn't know, when we talked before, that it
was Alex you were talking about.'

'How could you have known?' Geraldine shrugged. 'It
was my fault for being so secretive.'

'Likewise. I should have told you that Alex had been
the man in my life, and that we'd decided to give our
relationship another try.'

'Shall we just say it was a misunderstanding all
round?' said Geraldine.

'Yes,' said Sara. 'No hard feelings?' she added.

'No hard feelings,' Geraldine agreed, with a faint
smile. 'After all, we do all have to work together.'

'Quite.' Sara nodded. 'Geraldine, about Calvin...'

'What about Calvin?' she said sharply.

'Do you think there's a chance you might be able to
forgive him? To give your marriage another try?'

'I don't know, Sara. I'm really not sure. He hurt me
very badly, you know.'

'Yes, Geraldine, I know he did,' said Sara gently, 'just
as I'm sure he knows it as well...but life really is very
short.'

'I know.' Geraldine sighed. 'We've agreed to talk. To
try and see why our marriage went wrong. I can't make

any promises at this stage but, well, I suppose talking is a start.'

'I'd say it's a very good start,' said Sara. 'Alex and I have had to do a lot of talking to see why our relationship floundered when it did.'

'Have you come to any conclusions?' asked Geraldine curiously.

'Oh, yes,' said Sara. 'There simply wasn't enough give and take, but now, well, I hope we've sorted a lot of things out.'

'What will happen here?' asked Geraldine after a moment. 'After the baby is born, I mean? Does Francis know yet?' she went on, as if the thought had only just struck her.

Sara smiled. 'Yes, he knows.'

'Whatever did he say?'

'Well, he was a bit taken aback at first, to say the least, but I think we've sorted out solutions that will suit everyone. Henry Jackson is going to do some extra locum duties to cover my maternity leave. I intend to return to work, but only on a part-time basis. If Henry doesn't want to cover that, it's been decided to bring in further help.'

'What about the baby when you're at work?'

'Jean has offered to help out. You know how she loves children—especially babies—and how much she misses her own grandchildren. She says that helping with my baby will be the next best thing and that it'll give her something to do until Francis retires in a few years' time.'

'So all's well that ends well?' said Geraldine, and again the wistful look was back in her eyes.

'Yes,' said Sara. 'I suppose you could say that.'

'Isn't it incredible how much can change in such a short space of time?' said Sara, sitting up and hugging her knees as she gazed out across the breathtaking views of the countryside.

'You mean since the last time we were up here?' Alex raised his head, propped himself on one elbow and began to chew a stem of grass.

'Yes,' said Sara, warily watching Jason who was frantically searching for rabbits amongst the hillocks and gorse bushes of the downland. 'Then I didn't know where I was going. I didn't even have a job, and now my whole future seems mapped out for me. Not only am I a partner in a reputable group practice, I'm also about to be married and motherhood is just around the corner.'

'And very soon you'll be up to your ears in brickdust and rubble,' said Alex with a chuckle.

'You spoke to the builder?' She turned her head to look at him.

'Yes.' Alex nodded. 'He doesn't seem to think there'll be too much trouble with the conversion of the cottages. The living-rooms can be knocked into one large area, as can the kitchens, and upstairs there'll be ample room for a nursery and a guest room. He did say there'd be quite a bit of upheaval so I had a word with Jean and Francis and they said we could stay at Marshcombe House while it was all going on.'

'They've been marvellous,' said Sara. 'My own parents couldn't have done more for me.' Once again she found she had a huge lump in her throat.

'Are you happy?' asked Alex. 'Or has it all been too sudden?'

'Yes,' she said, 'I am happy. Very happy. And, yes, it has been sudden,' she admitted. 'At times I think I must be dreaming, that I'll wake up and find none of it's real. I think some of the others at the centre have been a bit taken aback as well by the speed of events.'

'Ah, but what none of them knew was just how far

you and I had gone before. All we've done now is to confirm things.'

'I did speak to Geraldine,' she said quietly.

'What did she say?'

'She was fine about things, actually. She understood.'

'Good. I'd hate to have been the cause of any more pain for her,' said Alex. 'Especially when I'd only been trying to cheer her up in the first place and make things better.'

'She seemed,' Sara said after a moment, 'somehow wistful about us...especially about the baby.'

'She told me once that she regretted she and Calvin not having children. I think she felt that things might have been different if they had.'

'Well, who knows? Maybe they'll have another try at their marriage, and with all this talk of babies...'

'Talking of mothers and children,' said Alex suddenly, as if something had just occurred to him, 'I spoke to the consultant at St Benedict's this afternoon about young Liam Turvey.'

'Oh?' Sara turned quickly and looked at him again. 'What did he say?'

'The tests were all OK—his spine wasn't broken. His other injuries will all heal in a matter of time.'

'That must have been a tremendous relief for Linda,' said Sara. They both fell silent for a while. All that could be heard was the high-pitched singing of crickets in the long grass and the distant bleating of sheep, the ordinary familiar sounds of a drowsy summer's evening.

'You know, Alex,' Sara went on at last, 'there's so much more to this whole business of being a parent than I'd ever realised.'

'You can say that again,' he agreed. 'I think the last few weeks have taught us that. It's frightening, really. I just hope we're never put to the sort of test that Marilyn

Jones had to face or Linda Turvey or—come to that—
even poor old Joyce Webster.'

'You think you'd never cope,' said Sara, 'but I guess
when you're faced with these situations you just do.'

'There has to be another side to it as well,' said Alex.

Sara smiled. 'You mean sleepless nights, nappies and
teething?'

'I was thinking more along the lines of rugby matches,
train sets and fishing.'

'It might be a girl,' Sara protested.

'She might like rugby, trains and fishing... All right,
then, how abut first smiles, cuddles, Sunday mornings in
bed and dressing up as Father Christmas?' said Alex with
a grin. He reached out and pulled her down beside him
in the little hollow in the grass.

'It's going to be wonderful, Alex,' she said, running
her finger down his cheek and then pushing his hair back
from his forehead. 'Just you and me and the baby.'

'True,' he murmured, leaning forward slightly and nib-
bling her earlobe, 'but until then it's just you and me,
and we have a honeymoon to think about.'

'Did you have anywhere in mind?'

'I've always fancied the Seychelles myself,' he replied.
'All those waving palms, white sand and blue sea.'

'That sounds wonderful,' she replied. 'Actually, anywhere would be wonderful...with the possible exception
of Saudi.'

'True.' He smiled. 'You know something? I was all
set to go there once.'

'Really?' She looked at him in surprise. 'When was
that?'

'A few months ago,' he admitted. 'I was coming out
to see you, to talk to you. You see, I couldn't stand it
any more. I couldn't believe we'd thrown everything
away. I was in the process of arranging a flight when we

heard you were coming home.' He paused, then asked curiously, 'Was it only the heat that forced you home?'

'Not really,' she replied sheepishly. 'Actually I couldn't stand it any longer either. I knew I'd made a mistake almost as soon as I got there. I missed you so much, Alex,' she whispered, 'but I didn't want to admit it—even to myself.'

'Then why were you so prickly with me when you first came home?'

'I wasn't prickly!' she protested. She caught sight of his expression and said, 'Well, perhaps I was, just a bit…but I didn't know how you were feeling and I didn't want to take the risk of it all falling apart again.'

'And I was afraid of rushing you. I was terrified that if I declared my true feelings I'd simply scare you away again.'

They were silent again. From the nearby gorse bushes there came a scrabbling sound, followed by a short, ecstatic bark. They both smiled. Bending his head, Alex said softly, 'It seems we both have an awful lot of time to make up for.'

'That's all right,' Sara replied, lifting her face for his kiss, 'because now we know we've got the rest of our lives in which to do it.'

MILLS & BOON®

Makes any time special

Enjoy a romantic novel from
Mills & Boon®

Presents™ Enchanted™ Temptation®

Historical Romance™ Medical Romance™

MILLS & BOON®

Medical Romance™

COMING NEXT MONTH

A TRUSTWORTHY MAN by Josie Metcalfe

Sister Abigail Walker thoroughly enjoyed her work in the A&E
department, even more so when Dr Ben Taylor arrived! But
was Ben the trustworthy and gentle colleague she thought
him to be…

BABIES ON HER MIND by Jessica Matthews

Midwife Emily Chandler had not intended to succumb to
obstetrician Will Patton. Just because she found herself
unexpectedly pregnant was no reason to marry him but Will
had other ideas!

OUR NEW MUMMY by Jennifer Taylor
A Country Practice—the second of four books.

Dr David Ross was unprepared for his reaction to the arrival
of Laura Mackenzie, consultant paediatrician. Was he
betraying the memory of his wife or was it time to move on…

TIME ENOUGH by Carol Wood

Dr Ben Buchan's new locum, Dr Kate Ross, was making a
determined effort to start her life again. But did that include
becoming involved with the boss?

Available from 4th June 1999

Available at most branches of WH Smith, Tesco, Asda,
Martins, Borders, Easons, Volume One/James Thin
and most good paperback bookshops